A Time for Tears

Jerelynn J. Henrikson

Meadowlark Press, LLC
Emporia, Kansas

Meadowlark Press, LLC
meadowlark-books.com
PO Box 333, Emporia, KS 66801

Copyright © 2020 Jerilynn Jones Henrikson

Cover photo by Duane Henrikson

Rachel's Diary illustrations by Elizabeth Daniel.

ISBN: 978-1-7342477-8-7

Library of Congress Control Number: 2020946233

A Time for Tears

Jerilynn Jones Henrikson

ALSO BY THIS AUTHOR

PICTURE BOOKS

Grandma's Prairie Patchwork . . . A Kansas Color Book

Raccoons in the Corn

Prairie Tales: The Wispers, Grones, and Ponders

Bad Cat!

Desert Dreadfuls (or....Maybe Not!)

JOE THE GARDENER SERIES OF EARLY READERS

Level 1: No Weeds, No Bugs, No Bunnies

Level 2: Seeds, Leaves, Fruits, and Roots

Level 3: Joe and Pam Make Jam

YA HISTORICAL FICTION

Teddy the Ghost Dog of Red Rocks

ADULT MEMOIR

Seven to One: My Life Measured in Dog Years

for Victims of
War and Prejudice

Table of Contents

Historical Characters

This story is a work of historical fiction. Although the places and some of the events are real, most of the characters and situations are fiction. The following persons are real, historical figures:

William Allen White: newspaper editor from Emporia, Kansas, author, political activist, friend of presidents, who served as Chairman of the Committee to Defend America by Aiding the Allies before America entered WWII.

Franklin D. Roosevelt: 32nd president of the United States from 1933 until his death in 1945.

Winston Churchill: Prime Minister of England from 1940-1943 and again from 1950-1955. He was also the founder of the SOE or Special Operations Executive, the ultra-secret organization designed to assist the French Resistance defeat Hitler's Nazis.

Charles de Gaulle: French General, head of the French Army and the French Government in Exile in Britain.

Adolf Hitler: Chancellor and Führer of Germany from 1933-1945 and head of the Nazi Party. Perpetrator of "The Final Solution," a plan to exterminate the Jews of Europe.

Dwight Eisenhower: US Army five-star general, Supreme Commander of the Allied Expeditionary Force in Europe, planner and supervisor of the invasion of Normandy 1944-1945, and President of the United States 1953-1961.

General George Patton: Commander of USA's Third Army in WWII.

General Erwin Rommel: perhaps Germany's most brilliant commander in WWII.

Eric Piquet-Wicks: organizer and recruiter for the SOE.

Klaus Barbie: German SS and Gestapo officer, known as the Butcher of Lyon for his treatment of Jews and members of the Resistance.

André Trécomé: pastor and leader of the peaceful resistance movement in Le Chambon-sur-Lignon, France, the village in the Haute Loire Region of France that saved thousands of Jews.

Fictional Characters

The following persons are characters in this story, based on the author's imagination.

Soissons, France

Henri Jabot: ten-year-old boy killed during a German bombing raid of Soissons.

André Jabot: Henri's oldest brother who becomes one of the Resistance's most deadly saboteurs. Also a member of the SOE. The Shadow.

Charlotte Jabot: mother of Henri and André .

Topeka, Kansas, USA

Daniel Hagelman: Jewish grocer from Topeka, KS. Volunteers for British Royal Air Force in 1939. Selected for the Special Operations Executive (SOE), Prime Minister Winston Churchill's secret organization of spies and saboteurs in WWII. Resistance member.

Ida Hagelman: Daniel's wife and Maggie's mother.

Maggie Hagelman: Daniel's daughter who is born the day he leaves for war.

Jacob and Berta Hotzel: Daniel's cousins, refugees from Germany, come before WWII to escape Nazi persecution and help run the family grocery store.

Sarah Hagelman: Daniel's mother, helps run the store and raise Maggie.

Paris, France

Rachel Ropfogel/Simone Bouret: fifteen-year-old Jewish school girl whose parents send her to the South of France to escape Hitler's persecution where she becomes . . .

Simone Bouret, Resistance member, art teacher.

Benjamin Ropfogel: Rachel's father, a banker in Paris.

Esther Ropfogel: Rachel's mother and a successful portrait artist.

On the Train to Le Chambon-sur-Lignon, France

Clarine Auguste: fellow traveler with son Jacques and daughter Baby Marie.

Fredrik Haught: SS Nazi Jew hunter, sadist, killer.

Le Chambon-sur-Lignon, France

Lily DeBauge: Resistance member, friend to Simone.

Madame Lawrence: Boarding house owner, Resistance member, Marie's caretaker.

Doctor Mason: Local physician who saves Daniel.

Lyon, France

Alice Upstill: SOE operative, wireless expert.

Bertie MacIntosh: SOE munitions expert.

Aunt Lucile DeBauge: Resistance cell leader, safe-house operator.

Rachel's Map

Inspiration in Old Vienne

Misty rain came and lifted as I rested on an iron bench,
enjoying the soft atmosphere of damp, narrow passages
hugging the hillside.

Then I saw her, the tallest lady in France.

Her bold strides across the cobbles
Revealed a blue dress beneath her open raincoat.
She wore a wide black hat and high-heeled shoes.

Graceful, confident, tall, and narrow,
she smiled down at me
and marched on, across those crippling cobbles.

She strode past.
From the back, her wild silver curls
submitted to an audacious yellow bow.
She carried ninety years with ease.

Is that yellow ribbon a defiance
of distant or present persecutions?
Are the heels on cobbles a revolt to advancing age?
Is *la Résistance* in her bones?

How would such a woman react
to recent images that haunt my mind
of innocence captured in cages,
and the resulting ruin such caging brings?

And so was planted in my heart this seed
I have been coaxing for years.
I'm willing those who harvest any blossoms
to be moved to action by her tears.

And So the Story Begins . . .

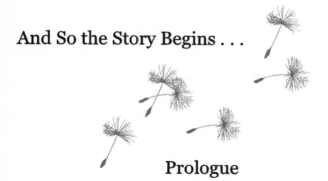

Prologue

World War II began in France for a group of children and their teacher in 1940 on a May afternoon in a field near the town of Soissons not far from Paris. On days when the weather was fine, this teacher often led her students from the school to a nearby meadow to have their lunch of baguette with butter, ham, and cheese. After lunch they would walk in the meadow, identifying plants, insects, and birds. This particular day, one of the boys, Henri Jabot, age ten, made a startling discovery in the trees at the verge of the field: a wrecked airplane camouflaged with branches.

"Madame Rosseau!" he shouted to the teacher. "Here is an airplane. I think it is British!" Everyone ran to pull away the branches so they could see what proved to be the wreck of a British glider.

Just then they heard the roar of another aircraft approaching. Streaking in low, black crosses marking its wings, the plane was quickly upon them. At first, teacher and children stood frozen in awe of the noise and speed of the aircraft. Too late, Henri, recognizing the danger, shouted, "RUN!" The pilot strafed the screaming children with staccato bursts from the wing-mounted machine guns and disappeared over the trees beyond the grass and wildflowers. Did the pilot mistake the children for the crew of the downed glider? Did he think them to be British commandos? Perhaps he was simply a mindless cog in the German war machine that was at that moment blitzing terror upon the people of Soissons. Regardless of this pilot's motivation, Henri and five of the other thirteen children were killed. The teacher and two more were wounded.

In a matter of days, France surrendered. The terror of this attack had brought about its intended effect by forcing France to surrender or see every settlement in France so destroyed.

There was, however, an additional unintended effect. The destruction of Soissons and more pointedly the death of young Henri Jabot inspired his oldest brother André, then age seventeen, to transform himself into a deadly shadow with a hundred faces and as many names. He became France's most effective, elusive, and deadly saboteur.

PART I

War

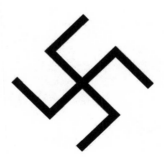

The swastika is an ancient symbol used by many religions over time. It was a symbol of good luck and prosperity. Adolf Hitler rose to power in Germany and used it as the symbol of the Nazi party. Today it continues to be associated with white supremacy and racism.

CHAPTER 1:
Introductions

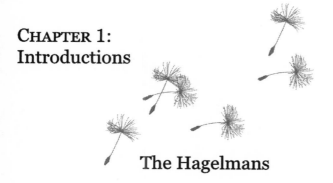

The Hagelmans

The war began for the Hagelman family in Kansas in 1939 when Daniel made the decision to leave his family. Newborn daughter Maggie was just minutes old when he left her, his wife Ida, and their home above their grocery store in Topeka, Kansas, to travel to England to volunteer with British forces to help defeat Hitler.

Daniel's grandparents had left Germany to eventually settle in Topeka two generations before, when anti-semitism drove them from Heidelberg, where they operated a kosher meat market in the Jewish quarter. In 1935, more Hagelman relatives came from Berlin as the Nazi threat to Jews became increasingly ominous. Long evenings of serious discussion among new arrivals, Cousins Berta and Jacob Hotzel, and Ida and Daniel, brought sharp focus to the evil that was brewing in Germany. "Adolf Hitler und hees Nazis are devils," Cousin Berta declared. "Hees thugs come in night to bookshop next door to our market, throw stones through vindows, burn books in street. They break vindows in our market und steal meat, butcher tools, wreck everyting. Jews not safe on streets. Hitler lie about us. Ve not lif in dirt or haf sickness. Ve not steal babies to make Jewish."

"Yes," Jacob added, "und verse, so many Germans belief dees lies: "Jews steal our wealth, Jews sell us out in the Great War. Our German friends and neighbors turn against us."

"Dere are stories of labor camp und Jews taken avay in middle of night, never to be see again," Berta added. "Und verst of all, many Americans not vant us here. Tank God ve haf you to come to!"

Every Saturday at temple, at coffee or lunch in the local deli, around dinner tables, the Jewish community in Topeka spoke with growing concern about the horrors of Hitler's antisemitism. Other strong voices spoke out about the necessity of opposing Hitler's policies. One evening on the radio, the Hagelmans heard the editor of *The Emporia Gazette*, a small-town newspaper in Emporia, just fifty miles south of Topeka. That editor, William Allen White, Progressive friend of former President Teddy Roosevelt, influenced Daniel with his words. As Chairman of the Committee to Defend America by Aiding the Allies, White described the Nazi threat by saying,

> "It stands just beyond our borders waiting. What your sacrifices will be, what hardships you may meet, what anguish you may know, I cannot prophesize. I only know unless that beast is chained upon the fields of France, your lives will be maimed and mangled by its claws."

White's warning and the experiences of Daniel's own family convinced him to act, to do what he could to help stop Hitler's assault upon human decency. "I know Americans are struggling to do the right thing," Daniel stated one evening at dinner. "The Isolationists want us to stay out of the fighting. That's understandable. So many died in the Great War. Memories of thousands dying of disease and mustard gas in the trenches remain vivid. They think the broad oceans will keep us safe, but modern aeroplanes and U-boats can reach us. Meanwhile thousands are suffering. My heart breaks to leave you, Ida, and our little child, but I must go to keep my country, my people, and you—my family—from harm."

Daniel would make his decision in March of 1939. The Japanese, allies of Hitler's German Reich, made the decision for America on December 7, 1941, when they launched their deadly attack on Pearl Harbor in Hawaii. By then, Daniel Hagelman was already in Lyon, France with a British commando unit helping the French Resistance.

The Ropfogels

The war began for Rachel Ropfogel and her parents in Paris as the Nazis invaded in May of 1940. Adolph Hitler lusted after Paris as another man might desire a beautiful woman. He hoped to avoid destroying Paris as he was attempting to destroy London and had already leveled Poland. He wanted to possess it. He envied the Parisians their stylish way of life: elegant clothes, lively nightlife, fine food, and wine (or, as the French would say, their *joie de vivre*). He planned to possess their city of Gothic cathedrals, grand palaces, art museums, and block after block of wedding cake buildings, to make them part his dream of a grand world Reich. He began a campaign of terror and propaganda to convince political and military leaders of France that his proposal for surrender was their only logical choice.

For twenty years Rachel's father, Benjamin Ropfogel, had managed a successful bank in one of those lovely buildings of Paris. Her mother Esther painted portraits of prominent clients to hang in their homes. Esther had left New York in the 1920s to study art at the Sorbonne and met a handsome young banker at a professor's dinner party. She and Ben were married less than a year after they met, and daughter Rachel was born in April of 1925.

For many in Europe, the rumblings in Germany were easy to dismiss, but by the time Rachel was ten, Hitler was moving to gain power by rousing the German people with a fierce nationalism that pointed to Jews as the reason for all Germany's social, political, and economic problems, thus creating a convenient and effective scapegoat. Poland was blitzed, air bombardment of Britain began, and Hitler turned his greedy eye and his armies toward France. The onslaught of German forces overpowered the French army and its British allies, and by May of 1940, France surrendered. The result was a strange and uneasy peace, with Hitler's iron grip in firm control of Paris and the North of France, and a German-controlled puppet French government centered in Vichy in the South.

"Rachel, my child," her father announced one evening at supper, "we have begun seeking a way to move you from Paris to a safer place somewhere in the South." Her mother Esther smiled bravely, her large, dark eyes glistening with suppressed tears.

"But Papa," Rachel protested, "why can't we all go? I'm no longer a child; I'm practically grown. I should have a say in my future. We should stay together as a family."

"There is no room for argument here, Rachel. The government is in disarray. France will fall. Our army is exhausted from fighting in vain to save Poland, and our leaders are confused and indecisive. Jews are being watched. Antisemitism is a disease and many Frenchmen have caught it. When it comes to Jews, the Nazis have little respect for wealth, or mercy for old or infant. I refuse to risk your life, *ma chère*. Our decision is final. Your mission is to live, learn, and return to us when this brutality ends."

"You must be brave and smart," her mother added. "We pray that our prominence here will protect us. It may help that I was born in America and hold dual citizenship, but even if I could go, I would never leave your father. Always remember who you were, but be prepared to become another person with another name, perhaps a new life with another family. The prayers you say will always be heard. God will listen. He loves you as much as your father and I do. We will do everything in our power to find you when the war ends."

The Jabots

The war began for André Jabot and his family with the death of little brother Henri and five classmates on that field near their château north of Soissons. Henri's death would drive seventeen-year-old André to leave France to seek *Général* Charles De Gaulle, leader of the French Army, in exile in England.

Young Henri's mother, Madame Charlotte Jabot, stood with her four surviving boys and the servants in a semicircle about Henri's small grave. Her dark hair streaked with silver at the temples, aquiline profile, and erect carriage gave her an air of privileged confidence. "I am sorry, dearest Henri, that Le Curé Pascal cannot be here to guide your soul to heaven. Like you, he was killed in yesterday's bombing. It is up to us—your family—to say the prayers. We pray for your soul. We pray for your father, suffering as a German captive. We pray for France and for our people. We pray for ourselves. We pray for victory."

"You can pray, *Maman*," her oldest, André, added. "I intend to fight. I swear on dear Henri's life that I will not cry another tear until I have avenged his death and set France free. I will make myself into an assassin to hound the German war machine. I will become a shadow haunting Hitler's dreams. I will learn to fight without mercy, to kill and to be a leader of killers. I will not stop until this evil is defeated." After a deep breath, he added, "*Vivre la France!*" quietly, almost as a prayer.

Although at seventeen André was little more than a boy himself, his wiry, athletic build gave power to his words. His deep-set dark eyes dilated with anger. A wild shock of black hair, clenched fists, and the power of words made more intense by the soft timbre of his voice, silenced his mother and brothers. None of them doubted; not one questioned the strength of his intentions.

From the cemetery hill behind the château, the household saw columns of smoke rising from beyond the forest. The Jabot family had lived for generations in their elegant home north of Soissons. When the Panzers shook the earth and bombers dropped devastation from the sky upon Soissons the day of Henri's death, Charlotte decided they must flee. The morning following the funeral, she and the servants loaded boxes of provisions and her four remaining boys into the family auto and they fled south. When they approached the main road just before noon, they found a tangle of cars, horse-drawn buggies, hand carts, and wagons clogging the road and spilling into the fields.

André, driving the cumbersome touring car, announced, "This panic is useless. We have no plan. We have no destination in mind. How long will it be until we run out of fuel and food? We should turn around and go home."

"*Oui*, I think you are right, André," his mother admitted. "The road is impassable, and who knows what will happen when all these people run out of food? At home we at least have our gardens and cows and chickens." André found a spot where the ditch was wide and the ground firm enough to make the turn. They were forced to bounce along on the edge of the road for half an hour or so, then the southbound caravan thinned, and they drove unimpeded, home to the château.

A surprise awaited them. Troop carriers, officers' cars, even a few tanks were parked haphazardly in the wide gravel drive before the steps leading to the entrance. Each was marked with German insignias. As the family stepped from their vehicle, a German officer flanked by two armed infantrymen came from the entrance and down the steps. He made a bow as crisp as his uniform and announced, "Madame Charlotte Jabot? I am Otto Reber, of the Führer's Panzers division. We have commandeered your château as our headquarters. Your home is large. You and your children may remain in the south wing if you choose. We will not interfere as long as you remain in the house and on the grounds and keep clear of rooms occupied by officials of the Reich."

"*Bien sûr,* why would I object?" Charlotte hissed. "Your Reich has murdered my ten-year-old son, imprisoned my aging husband, invaded my home, and ravaged my country. Keep in mind I have a thorough inventory of our furnishings and other belongings. I would suggest you make it clear to your men that there will be no looting. I have close family in Germany. They have power that I will not hesitate to call upon. I insist that you allow me to take my portrait from the main hall and the other family portraits from the stairway. My husband commissioned this painting of me. I claim it and the other artwork from the château. My servants will also have access to the kitchen. If I were you, I would lock the door of whichever bed chamber you choose to defile each night and push a heavy bureau in front of it."

So it was that in just a matter of weeks, fifteen-year-old Rachel Ropfogel, Baby Maggie's father Daniel Hagelman, and Henri's brother, seventeen-year-old André Jabot, had each begun their separate journeys into the world of war.

Chapter 2:
Departures

Daniel to England

Her father's journey to England began the day Maggie was born, March 15, 1939. Daniel had planned his departure to take place three weeks after she was due. Unfortunately, babies do not read timetables. She was three weeks late. Ida's labor was long. For nearly thirty hours, Daniel sat by her side as she squeezed his hand with each contraction. The train taking Daniel to New York via Chicago was to leave the station in Topeka at 11:00 AM. The clock on the delivery room wall read 10:05.

Daniel told the doctor, "Please, Doc, Ida is exhausted, and I refuse to leave until I meet my baby. Isn't there something you can do?" The doctor used forceps to hurry the process. Daniel had about twenty minutes to hold his daughter before he left to catch his train. "Let's call her Maggie," he said, smiling through tears at Ida. Years later, in Maggie's imagination, she would see her Dada gazing lovingly into her little red face, curling her baby fingers around his thumb, kissing the forceps marks on her downy head. Throughout her childhood, Maggie's mother would tell her this story every night after prayers and before bed.

As Daniel sat musing on the train to Chicago, he could not help wondering if he would ever see his family again.

Neither could he help the lump in his throat or the tears welling in his dark eyes.

When Maggie was five days old, she and her mother returned to their crowded apartment above Hagelman's Market in Topeka. Grandmother Sarah Hagelman lived there as did cousins Jacob and Berta Hotzel. Grandma Sarah, Cousin Berta, and Momma were Baby Maggie's constant caretakers. Cousin Jacob joked that they changed her so often, she never got a chance to "vet her britches," and Jacob became a master of coaxing smiles with clever, German accented songs and stories. His favorite involved walking two fingers up her little leg and singing:

> *Dere vas a mon dat come along.*
> *He alvays sung dis leetle song.*
> *Hees pocket held dis leetle moous,*
> *That yump in Maggie's POOPALEOOSE!*

At this point, he would tickle her tummy button. She loved this game as a child, and in future years, she delighted her own children and grandchildren with the same words, pronounced just as Cousin Jacob had sung them to her.

The adults also managed the small store below. Customers were mostly neighbors, both Jewish and Gentile. Everyone appreciated the fresh produce and eggs from nearby farmers. Cousin Jacob trained as a butcher, and the local rabbi ensured that his meat was strictly Kosher. The Rainbow Bakery truck supplied the store with baked goods and a *Rainbow Bread* screen door advertisement. A dairyman from North Topeka brought in glass bottles of milk with thick cream floating at the top, fresh churned butter, and homemade cottage cheese. A colorful assortment of tempting penny candies in clear, gallon jars lined the counter at the perfect level to tempt every young customer who had the required penny clutched in a fist or tied into the corner of a hanky.

In those days, little grocery stores like Hagelman's flourished in nearly every neighborhood in America. Customers ran charge accounts and paid promptly at the end of each month, and regulars at Hagelman's would call 647 and put in orders by phone. The delivery boy, Charlie, would pack the order into his bike basket and pedal to their front door. He would even help old Mrs. Hooley, who lived just two blocks down, put her Post Toasties on the shelf.

"To this day," Maggie would say more than seventy years later, "I can close my eyes, take a deep breath, and imagine the mingled odors of pungent onions and garlic, earthy potatoes, fresh bread, dried herbs, sliced corned beef, and oiled wood floors: the perfume of Hagelman's Market."

Daniel wrote when he could. Not all his letters made it past the censors. With the first one that did, Ida surmised he sometimes slipped in coded messages, like "earning his wings."

30 April 1939
My Dear Ones,
   I'm sure you know that this letter will be censored, so don't be surprised if portions of it are blacked out. I will be telling you about me, not about places or training, or even the names of my pals. First, I love

you all and miss you like crazy! One thing I am sure of, no matter how this war turns out, Adolf Hitler and his gang will rot in hell.

I hope that by leaving you to come here to join this fight, I am earning <u>my</u> heavenly wings and will someday glide into paradise...ha. You would laugh if you could see me, Ida my love. I have grown a moustache. My buddies say it makes me look "dashing" whatever that means.

If you want to send a care package, American cigarettes are much appreciated here, and I can use them to repay many kindnesses of shared goodies the "blokes" bring back from leave. Their "mums" are almost as good at baking as you, Mom. My favorite is "spotted dick." Now, Jacob, get your mind out of the gutter . . . it's a sort of raisin bread. I hate the Brit's version of toothpaste, so send me some Pepsodent and a new toothbrush.

I have developed a taste for warm beer and I even like Guinness. Don't worry now, I'm not spending all of my time or pay in the pub. Only been four times. Of course, I would love some cookies (they call them biscuits here)...peanut butter would be perfect. In fact, a whole jar of peanut butter would be great. These guys have never tasted it. Let's hear it for George Washington Carver and sliced bread. I'm sure the local strawberry jam would make a great peanut butter and jelly sandwich..

The Brits are a "lovely lot," friendly and generous. And England is a beautiful place, much greener than Kansas. There are flowers everywhere and I have not seen a single grasshopper. No mosquitoes either. Everyone seems to like Americans. The lady at the sandwich shop calls me "dearie" or "luv." They like Glen Miller records and Esther Williams movies, and really "dig jazz." I think everyone has a dog.

Most of my time is spent training and working hard. There are many serious things to learn—things that lives may depend on. Our enemy is strong, ruthless, and prepared, so we must be as well. I could not do this work if I did not feel God is on our side.

Ida, please don't cut your hair, I love it long. Give Maggie hugs and kisses from Dad and tell her every day, every minute, how much I love her. Write me soon and fill me in on all that's going on in the neighborhood. Hope the store is doing well, but I know you all will see to that. Send pictures. Pray for me. Pray for us all. *L'chaim,* my loves, *l'chaim.*

All my love, hugs, and kisses, Daniel

PS. Throw in some packs of gum and some Milk Duds.

PPS. They call diapers "nappies" or "napkins." Can you imagine putting a napkin on Maggie's fanny?

PPPS. I don't feel we had a proper good-bye. It was all so rushed. Be assured that when this is over, we will all have one hell of a proper hello.

Ida saved his letters in a lacquered wooden box she kept in a drawer in a table beside her bed, and she and Maggie re-read them year after year on Daniel's birthday.

Paris Falls

At dawn on June 14, 1940, Rachel Ropfogel and her parents Ben and Esther peered from one of their upstairs windows as German troops marched into Paris. By the terms of surrender, the French army withdrew to avoid violence to the city and its people. Citizens had been warned in advance and the streets were empty, shops shuttered. The Ropfogels and all their neighbors, indeed most citizens of Paris, made sure the windows and doors of their homes were closed and locked. The usual bustle of bicycle bells and taxi horns was replaced by the rumble of tanks and the pounding of goose-stepping German infantry marching past the *Arc de Triomphe* and down the *Champs-ÈlysÈes*.

The terms of the French surrender to Germany included:

- German control of all French ports on the Atlantic

- Three-fifths of French territory, including Paris and the northern territories

- 400,000 French francs per day to be paid by France to Germany for the occupation

- Return of all German refugees (Jews, primarily) and captured French soldiers to be used as slave labor (or sent to the death camps)

- The remainder of France was to be governed by a puppet, German-controlled "French" government in Vichy, a town in southern France.

The surrender was a blow to the pride of most French citizens. The most notable exception to that loss of pride belonged to those who joined the Resistance. On the other hand, some Frenchmen actively assisted the Germans including counter spy Resistance infiltrators and the paramilitary French Nazis known as *la Milice*, and some French citizens were forced to collaborate to survive as war is seldom a black or white situation. Resistance required stealth, bravery, intelligence, and luck; collaboration was sometimes the only means of survival.

Not all of the citizens of Paris were unsympathetic to the plight of their Jewish neighbors. In fact, although thousands of French Jews were killed by the Nazis, seventy-five percent of the Jews of Paris survived the war. Many of these were saved by non-Jewish friends and neighbors.

Day by day, week by week, the Nazis chipped away at the rights of the Jews of France, indeed, all Jews of the areas of Europe under their control. The arrests of targeted individual Jews began almost immediately, and general roundups or *rafle* began in 1941. The first trainload of Jews left Paris for the death camp at Auschwitz in July of 1942. Nazi propaganda encouraged citizens of Paris to turn in their Jewish neighbors and anyone who might be part of the Resistance. The Germans offered 10,000 francs as reward.

Any act of resistance resulted in arrest and almost certain death. The Nazis controlled all newspapers, radio broadcasts, even movies and public entertainments. The only source of real information passed from person to person, and word of Vichy collaboration or the Battle of Britain made the rounds in coffee shops or around dinner tables. Shortages of food, in Paris especially, increased as the Germans confiscated produce and meat. Parisians starved while Germans feasted. With Vichy assistance, many manufactured goods were directed to the German war machine.

At first, many prominent Jews in Paris hoped their long-standing social positions and successful businesses would protect them. They thought of themselves as thoroughly French. Yes, they were of Jewish descent, but generations of intermarriage had diluted the genetic links to their ancient past. Many did not practice the Jewish religion according to the strictest traditions. Unlike the Jewish refugees from Belgium, Germany, and

Poland, the Jews of Paris spoke perfect French with a proper Parisian accent. Within a month of the German occupation, it became obvious that the Jews of Paris were as much at risk as any of the Jewish refugees or Orthodox Jews wearing yarmulkes on their heads or prayer shawls under their jackets.

Rachel to Le Chambon-sur-Lignon

Ben and Esther Ropfogel were anxious to act on their plan to get Rachel out of Paris, hopefully to be safe with her protectors in the remote forested high plateau surrounding the village of Le Chambon-sur-Lignon. Preparations for young Rachel's journey would take several weeks. One evening at dinner her father said, "Rachel, the plan is for you to make the trip alone by train to Lyon. We will take advantage of your height and maturity well beyond your fifteen years. We count on your character to be as mature as your physical appearance. I have acquired forged papers that identify you as Simone Bouret, an art student from Lyon. Your cover story will be that you have been here in Paris, studying drawing and painting from Madam Esther

Ropfogel, renowned portrait artist. From Lyon, you will transfer to another train to Le Chambon-sur-Lignon where you will be teaching art at a Huguenot school. The people of this village are Godly people, and they do their good work in His name. You must never feel you are taking advantage of them because I have sent money to support their school. These funds will also extend to cover your room and board. I know that you will be an excellent teacher and find ways to be useful to their cause."

Her mother added, "While teaching there, you will live in your own room at a small boarding house, have access to the village, be a part of the local protestant congregation. You will be safest if you maintain an aloof demeanor until you are absolutely sure of the people you meet. I have prepared a secret pouch. In addition to the money it contains, you will find a folded note telling you the name of a bank in Zurich, Switzerland, and the number of an account there. Whatever happens to us, if you survive, you will be well provided for with the funds from this account after the war."

A week before Rachel's scheduled departure to the South, Esther invited her friend, Mimi Blanc, to come to lunch and to bring her scissors. Mimi, a skilled beautician, had styled Esther's hair for many years. She agreed to cut Rachel's long, curly dark hair into a short, bouncy bob. The result transformed a lanky schoolgirl with braids into a slim, stylish young French woman. "I will do my own packing, Mother," Rachel stated flatly. "I know I must pack carefully: no extras, no frills. I have a list: toothbrush, tooth powder, hairbrush, underwear, pajamas, blouses, a warm sweater, tailored gray slacks, brown skirt, navy dress, walking shoes, and my diary and pencils. It all fits in this small bag."

"You have done well, my dear," her mother said. "Your disguise is perfect, but if you keep a diary, you must be careful not to reveal anything about your true identity. Your past could put you and your protectors in terrible danger if your diary fell into unfriendly hands."

"I know, Mother," she answered. "I hope someday to understand why people allow hate, war, and injustice. I will be careful, but I will also try to find ways to resist. Perhaps there will be a chance for me to help others who are separated from their families, isolated from the homes and people they love."

A few weeks later, on a misty morning in early June of 1940, twenty-year-old art student Simone Bouret left the studio of Madame Ropfogel after bidding restrained good-byes from the front steps. Dressed in a long, somber raincoat, a dark suit, and black felt hat, she carried a shoulder bag with identification papers, ticket, cheese sandwich, and an apple. Her mother had sewn two pouches of cash and the Swiss bank information inside the shoulder pads of her coat. Clutching her valise, she stepped into the cab waiting at the curb and departed for the train station. Her quick backward glance from the car window caught her father's raised hand, and her mother's handkerchief, pressed to her cheek. This view of them burned into her memory. She knew the first entry into her diary would be a sketch of the scene. She would label the sketch, "My teacher and her husband" and sign it SB. She whispered a prayer that she would soon be home, and they would again be her beloved mother and father.

My teacher and her husband. SB

Rachel's Farewell

Rachel's escape from Paris began with a crush of passengers at the end of each railcar, pushing to board the train at Gare de Lyon Station in Paris. A Paris policeman thoroughly inspected each passenger's papers, and a uniformed railroad conductor punched each ticket. She found a seat by a window, placed her bag on the overhead rack, and settled into her place just as a stern-looking lady sat down next to her. A nervous young mother with a baby in arms and a toddler in tow took the seat facing them. With a cloud of steam and a long steam-whistle blast, the train began to chug from the station. The three-year-old boy, brown curls bouncing, clapped his hands and "woooo-wooooed" with the whistle as the train pulled away. The stern lady moved to a seat farther back. The young mother gave Rachel a shy smile.

Beneath Rachel's calm demeanor, her nerves stretched tight as bowstrings. She twined her fingers together across her middle to keep her hands from shaking. Soon enough, the train began to pass the suburbs of Paris and pick up speed. The clacking of wheels on rails and the swaying of the passenger car soothed her and she began to relax. The train plunged into misty rain as Rachel stared blankly out the window, and she began to see the drops sliding across the glass as tears. She smiled at the thought and renewed a silent pledge to keep her tears to herself. "When it is over, when it is over, then I will cry, then I will cry," became an internal chorus to the rhythm of the wheels.

The young mother in the facing seat interrupted Rachel's reverie to introduce herself. "Excuse me *Mademoiselle*, my name is Clarine Auguste. This is little Marie, and this bouncy one is my son Jacques. If you do not object, I would ask that Jacques sit beside you for a

Clarine, Jacques, and Baby Marie

time, so I can let Marie sleep here beside me on the seat.

"That will be fine," Rachel answered. "I am happy to have such a handsome companion." Little Jacques flashed her a dimpled grin and presented his hand for a handshake. His smile melted Rachel's natural reserve. "My, what a little gentleman. My name is Simone." She responded. "How old are you, Jacques?" Jacques held up three fingers, a feat that took both hands to raise the three fingers with thumb holding down the index finger.

"How ode you is?" Jacques asked. Rachel flashed ten fingers twice. "Woo, dat ode," observed Jacques.

From their seats toward the rear of the car, it was just a few steps to a built-in water station which included a wall-mounted spigot and cone-shaped paper cups. Jacques found the little cups and cool water irresistible. Rachel found herself helping him help himself. Then there would be the wobbly walk to the opposite end of the car to help him relieve himself in the tiny toilet, all complicated by the rocking motion of the moving train. With each trip, Clarine gave her new seatmate friend a grateful smile.

Before long, Marie awakened and Clarine wrapped them both in her shawl and began to discretely nurse the hungry infant. When Jacques, who had been nodding sleepily, crawled up beside his mother and sister and fell asleep, Rachel pulled her diary from her purse and began sketching them. She titled the drawing "Peace" and signed it SB.

From Paris to Lyon the tracks stretched just short of 500 kilometers, not a terribly long journey, but frequent stops to drop and pick up passengers and mail meant an all-day trip. At times the train followed the same path as the road south, and passengers could see a tangle of automobiles, groups of people walking, carrying bundles and bags, and carts with children perched atop belongings. Not everyone fleeing Paris could afford a train ticket. Not everyone fleeing Paris was a Jew, but Hitler and his Reich, with the aid of the Vichy police, quickly set about catching and deporting every Jew they could find northeast to press into slave labor or send to the death camps. Many Jews were desperately seeking a place to hide or a way out of France.

At midday almost every passenger produced a sandwich or apple or chunk of cheese from pocket or purse for a noon meal. Rachel's cheese sandwich was a bit squashed from its journey but tasted as good as any cheese sandwich she had ever eaten. She remembered her mother's words, "Hunger is the best spice," and she even enjoyed the crust. Thinking of her mother brought a stab of sadness and a pang of fear. Just what unknown challenges might lie ahead? She returned to her vow to take each problem as it came and not let fear dictate her decisions. Somehow she knew that calm calculation would be her best armor. She did not expect that armor to be tested quite so soon.

The train slowed and stopped at Dijon to let off some passengers and pick up mail bags, fill the water tank, and replenish the coal. Meanwhile two men presented their papers and tickets and came up the aisle looking for empty seats. Clarine handed little Marie over to Rachel, sat down next to her, and lifted Jacques onto her lap, then directed the men to sit across from them. One of the men looked to be in his seventies. The other was about forty and a younger version of the older: obviously father and son. The older gentleman's eyes shifted nervously about the car, looking from face to face. The younger placed his hand upon his father's knee, a gesture that seemed to calm and ease the older man's tension. They were both dressed tidily in work shirts, canvas pants, and sturdy shoes, but somehow their faces and hands seemed too smooth and well kept. They looked more like the hands of businessmen than tradesmen or laborers.

The younger man introduced himself and his father, "*Bonjour*, ladies. Thank you for making room for us. My father and I are traveling to Lyon to visit his sick mother, my grandmother. Papa has not traveled by train before and, as you can see, he is a bit nervous. My name is Armond and my father is Robert. I'm sure he will soon be his usual jovial self, and you will know a good deal more about us than you may think necessary." Both men smiled and nodded.

Much to the amusement of all, Jacques handled the introductions for their little party. He pointed to himself, "Jacques," then his little sister, "Mawee," then his mother, "Mama," then Rachel, "Dis Simoe, nize ode wady." Their laughter broke the ice, and they all began to chat. They had traveled but a few miles when suddenly the train began to slow, slow, slow, and gradually lurch to a full steam-hissing stop—no village, no station, in the middle of a quiet forest glade. Three men came striding in step along the tracks. A curve in the roadbed allowed Rachel a view of them, coming from the front of the train. Their long black automobile waited at a remote crossing near the engine. An electric current of fear ran from passenger to passenger. The men stopped beside the entry to their car, and the railway attendant hurried to open the door. Two wore the uniforms of the Vichy police. The third wore the unmistakable gray of a Nazi SS officer. Armond, his father Robert, and young Rachel stopped breathing.

André to England

J ust days after returning to the château, Charlotte began helping André organize his escape to England. "My son, in order to get training and support for this ambition to be a leader of *la Résistance*, you must make connections with the British military and *Général* Charles de Gaulle, leader of the Free French government and military, exiled in England." (Fine wine, excellent food, chic clothing, and connections had always been her *spécialité.*) Within three days, Charlotte had arranged for André to travel to Paris under the guise of continuing his education at university. In Paris, an engraver friend of hers would create false papers that would allow André to cross the border into Spain. "You will disguise yourself as a laborer fleeing south, blend in with that horde of refugees, and make your way to Spain," she explained. "My cousin, Manuel Vargas, works as a secretary at the

British Consulate in Madrid. Go directly there. Give him this letter. From there, he will know how to arrange transportation for you to London. He will also arrange a meeting with *Général* De Gaulle," his mother told him, her dark eyes sparkling passionately. "Take care, prepare yourself, make us proud."

"I will do my best to bring honor to our country," André replied.

After a harrowing journey across the Pyrenees into Spain, when he had finally convinced authorities there that he was neither a criminal nor a spy, he at last made connection with his mother's cousin at the embassy and was allowed to travel to Britain.

In Britain he also became entangled in suspicion and red tape. He was questioned by officials of M15 and M16, agencies in control of government security. At last he was brought before a rather unlikely leader of super spies, Lieutenant Eric Picquet-Wicks, who was the chief selection and training officer of the Special Operations Elective or SOE. Picquet-Wicks, a tall, thin, scholarly-looking man with an odd, curling smile and thick glasses, instinctively seemed to recognize in André the traits of a super spy. "So, young man," he addressed André, "what motivates you to be a leader with the Resistance?"

"Three generations of my family have served in the French military. My father Jean-Claude Jabot fought against the Germans with the French Army in Poland, was captured, and is now held in a German prisoner of war camp, if he is still alive. My ten-year-old brother was killed in the German blitz of Soissons. The German army has commandeered my family home and holds my mother and four brothers hostage. I intend to make contact with *Général* de Gaulle for his advice and blessing. I believe your agency will give me the training I require. I want to win the war for the Allies, but my heart is with my county and its citizens. My first loyalty lies with them. I believe the road to victory begins by first liberating France."

Much to André 's surprise, Picquet-Wicks replied by producing a tablet and pen and writing down directions to Carlton Gardens, de Gaulle's headquarters in London. This display of trust convinced André that joining the British and their SOE was the right path to accomplish his goals. "When you have met with him, return to me. I am sure I can equip you to be instrumental in winning this war." Picquet-Wicks dismissed him with a hand-shake and his quirky, tight-lipped smile.

CHAPTER 3:
Transformation

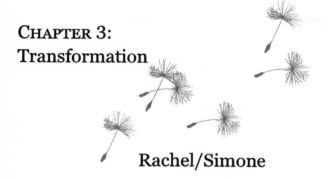

Rachel/Simone

The three officers pushed their way past the conductor and into the railroad car. Methodically they came up the aisle demanding each section stand and present identification papers and tickets, which they checked carefully. When they got to Rachel's little group, the SS officer, Fredrik Haught, checked her papers first. Hate twisted his handsome features into an evil sneer. His cold blue eyes scanned her face as he held out a demanding gloved hand. She was forced to shift Clarine's sleeping baby to one arm and fish her papers awkwardly from her purse. When Haught finished checking them, he pushed the packet back into her hand so forcefully that he knocked her down into her seat. Baby Marie was jarred awake; she and Jacques both began to cry. Haught leered at Clarine as he checked her papers.

"So, Frau Offerman, did you think you would escape us?" he growled into her face. "Your husband and older son are already packed with other criminals into cattle cars headed east. It appears that wealth and fame and forged papers will not protect you from the justice of the Reich. It would be a shame for the family to be separated.

You will accompany us from this train, and we will get you back where you and all Jewish criminals belong."

One of the Vichy policemen slung Jacques squirming and shrieking under his arm. The other wrenched Clarine's elbows behind her and pushed her down the aisle. They were outside in seconds, and the train began to move down the tracks away from them. As their train car passed her new friend, Rachel's eyes met Clarine's upturned gaze through the window. Outside from below she mouthed, "Thank you for saving my baby." The entire scene took not more than five minutes.

The passengers sat in stunned silence until Robert stood and shouted, "Filthy German fascist pigs!" And in that moment, Rachel's transformation was complete. She was no longer a fifteen-year-old Parisian schoolgirl. She was now and henceforth twenty-year-old Simone Bouret, art teacher, protector of Marie, and soon to be member of *la Résistance Française.*

Little Marie cried herself into an exhausted sleep. Simone was relieved to find diapers, bottles, tins of condensed milk, and several changes of clothes for the baby in the bag the woman she knew as Clarine had left behind on the rack above the seats. Her mind whirled as she imagined all the complications of caring for this child while adjusting to her new life in Le Chambon. Unsurmountable, unimaginable challenges, like wolves in a dark forest, loomed in her thoughts. Clarine's anguished face hung before her eyes as Jacques's screams echoed in her ears. Again she reminded herself that panic would not solve problems. She had to trust herself to deal with whatever came next, to overcome each complication as it presented itself. She must have confidence in her own strength and intelligence. Above all, she knew this was not the time for tears.

Slowly the images of recent horror were pushed back by present reality; the next hurdle would be dealing with the person her father had arranged for her to meet in Lyon and transport her to the village, Le Chambon-sur-Lignon. She did not know a name or even if her transporter would be a man or a woman, only that the person had been given her description and would approach her when she arrived. She was worried that she would not be recognized carrying a baby.

Clarine Captured

She turned to Armond. "I must ask a favor, Sir. When we arrive in Lyon, could you please help me off the train by carrying the baby? I will manage the luggage, but I cannot handle her as well. More importantly, the person meeting me is a stranger who may not recognize me by the description he or she has been given if I am carrying this child. I must trust you not to ask questions. After all we have witnessed today, I ask you to help me without knowing my full story. When I have assured the person who I am, he or she can help me with Marie on the next leg of our journey."

"Of course I will help you," he answered. "You are brave to take on this poor child. God bless you and be with you both in these difficult times. I do not need to know your story as you do not need to know mine. My father and I will pray for you both."

Evening was approaching as the train pulled into Lyon. A third or more of the passengers had reached their destination and the platform was fairly crowded as Simone and Robert stepped down from the train. Robert's son Armond followed, carrying Baby Marie. A group of Vichy policemen were observing the departing passengers and randomly checking papers. Their attention did not fall upon Simone and her friends, who passed by and walked slowly toward the station looking for someone who seemed to be searching for Simone. Just before they reached the impressive stone building, a young woman approached and asked, "*Pardon*, but are you Simone Bouret?" Simone nodded yes. "I am here from the College Cevenol International to transport you to Le Chambon and get you settled in your room. My name is Lily DeBauge, and I teach at the college. My aunt lives just a few blocks from the station here in Lyon. We will stay with her tonight and catch the local train to Le Chambon at eight tomorrow morning."

"I am so happy to meet you, Lily," Simone answered. "I would like you to meet my two travel friends, Robert and Armond. This is my baby, Marie," she said, taking the infant from Armond's arms. "I know no one expected me to have a child, yet here she is, and I hope you all will welcome both of us."

"Well, this is a surprise," Lily answered. "But there is no need to worry. Many staff and faculty at the school have children, and there are three other single mothers. So many young men have died in the fighting. Madame Lawrence who owns the boarding house where your room is located looks after a set of two-year-old twin boys. I'm sure she will welcome Baby Marie into her little brood of chicks."

Simone turned to the two men. "Thank you both and bless you. Goodbye. I will never forget you." In turn, they each hugged Simone and kissed her cheeks.

"Our prayers go with you, Simone. May you live to see a life of peace where no child lives in fear or is threatened by violence," Robert said.

"Amen," Armond added in agreement. As the two of them turned and walked into the station, Simone snapped a mental picture. Before she fell asleep that night, she added three drawings to her notebook. One of them portrayed the two men, arm in arm, walking toward the train station. She labeled it "Two Good Men." The second was of Baby Marie, tummy full of milk, swaddled in a soft blanket, asleep on a pallet on the floor beside her bed. She labeled it "Rest." The third was a close-up of Clarine's anguished face looking up to her from below the train. She labeled it "Pain."

Early the next morning Lily's Aunt Lucile fixed *crêpes* with berries and tiny steaming cups of espresso for breakfast. Marie chugged her bottle. "She seems to understand the importance of being an easy baby," Lily observed.

"Oh, yes," Simone responded. "I'm afraid I know next to nothing about babies. It seems that Marie is happy if her bottom is dry, and her tummy is full. I hope she continues to be so easily satisfied!"

By eight o'clock, they had walked the three blocks to the train station and were in a short line of passengers waiting to board the quaint little train that would carry them through the mountains to Le Chambon-sur-Lignon. Again a Vichy official checked papers and a railway employee punched tickets.

These train cars were different from the cars of the main line. Again rows of seats faced each other, but these were of wooden slats, no upholstery, and much narrower than the more modern train. The only other passengers in the car were an elderly couple who chose seats at the opposite end from their little party. Wooden racks above the benches, like little roofs, enclosed the pairs of seats. Simone, with Marie in her lap, took one side, and Lily sat facing them. A large sliding window provided a view of the passing countryside. A narrow aisle stretched from one end of the car to the other between the rows of seats. As the blast of the steam whistle from the chunky little engine announced its departure, Simone felt a catch in her throat and tears began to burn behind her eyes. She remembered Jacques, hooting with that other train whistle, ages ago yesterday morning. How could it have been just yesterday morning?

"What is it?" asked Lily. "What is wrong?"

"I am fine," answered Simone. "I will explain completely later. For now, let's just say I have a cinder from the smokestack in my eye. For now, let's just enjoy this clackety ride through a beautiful countryside." Just a few kilometers outside Lyon, an impressive home caught her attention. It stood on the far side of the Rhône River, near the small town of Vienne. Pink stucco walls glowed in the morning sun as the peaked roof reached for the clouds. A slim turret surely held a spiral staircase. Simone's gaze followed the house and its surrounding landscape until the tracks turned into the forest, and it slipped from view. She immediately snatched up her diary and made a rough sketch of the house. Somehow she sensed a link to this dreamlike place had been forged into the chain of events that led toward her future.

As the train left the river basin and turned toward the east, lush stands of oak, chestnut, maple, locust, and pine alternated with open fields, where for centuries farmers had grown grapes, lavender, rows of vegetables, and raised goats and cattle. These open fields had attracted the attention of Resistance fighters and the Allied Special Service Forces infiltrators as places where men, weapons, food, and wireless radio equipment could be dropped by air. The narrow-gauge train wound through valleys and between rugged mountains.

Marble-white Charolais cattle grazed green pastures where streams flowed from the hills above. Occasionally a road big enough for automobile traffic crossed the tracks, but the picturesque villages were linked primarily by ancient dirt roads and the railroad. It seemed that every village claimed its own church with its tall steeple. Stone buildings lined cobbled streets. Cozy stone cottages clustered near the towns, many with orchards as side yards that provided apricots and apples. Sometimes a centuries-old château or monastery guarded the town from a nearby mountainside, or remains of an ancient arched bridge partially spanned a river and seemed to echo the marching steps of long dead Roman soldiers.

Simone struggled to lose herself in the passing beauty, but suppressed tears continued to sting her eyes as she grieved for the defeat of her country, its culture, and its people. She took a handkerchief from her bag, blew her nose, shook her head, and vowed to put all her will into stopping the tears and her enemies. "What has become of our revolution's battle cry of "*Liberté, Égalité, Fraternité*?" she whispered to herself.

Marie distracted her by giving the little grunt that announced she was hungry and needed her diaper changed. "I'll fix the bottle," Lily volunteered. "You change the pants!" They shook hands.

"I think we will be great friends," Lily added with a smile. She leaned forward in her seat, reached across and took Simone's two hands in her own. Pulling her close, she said softly, "I also think it is time for you to trust me. I know your story. I know your name is not Simone Bouret. I know your true identity is Rachel Ropfogel, and you are a Jew. Your father made the arrangements for you to come to Le Chambon-sur-Lignon. He had heard of the willingness of this Huguenot community to help refugees and, most particularly, Jewish children. I know you are not twenty years old, only fifteen."

Simone sighed with relief and answered, "Still I must explain that Marie is not my baby. Her mother and three-year-old brother Jacques were snatched off the train by the SS just north of Lyon. I was holding Marie, so the SS officer assumed she was my baby. From what he said, I concluded that her mother was an important artist or performer. He told her that her husband and other son had been caught and deported to a camp in Poland, and that she and Jacques would be joining them. The venom in that officer's voice and the ice of his blue-eyed gaze lead me to believe they are all four already dead."

"It is good that you trust me," Lily answered. "I am a courier for *la Résistance*, and daughter of the man your father contacted to make arrangements for your safe-keeping in Le Chambon until our side defeats the Germans. And it will happen. God is on our side. We Huguenots feel that it is our duty to help God's chosen people. And you need not worry about Baby Marie. You and I have already fallen in love with her, and Madame Lawrence will be excellent help. She will never suffer for a lack of mothering."

The train wound its way through the valley to the little town of Le Chambon-sur-Lignon nestled on the bank of the Lignon River in the Haute Loire region of south central France. The charming station house sat just one street off the main square. A central plaza near the river featured a community building, a church, a tavern and restaurant, and several shops. The town was inhabited mostly by French Calvinist Protestants known as Huguenots. Long persecuted by the Catholic majority, they created a haven of tolerance for others suffering from discrimination. This location, isolated by severe

winters, poor roads, and independent religious traditions, gave locals a quiet reserve that historically
provided an attitude of acceptance. Refugees from the
Spanish Civil War, those suffering from tuberculosis,
Jews fleeing the Germans; locals quietly welcomed and
protected those seeking refuge.

Madame Lawrence's boarding house, like most of the
buildings in the region was built long ago from the dark
granite of the surrounding mountains, and like most, it
was topped with distinctive red tiles. It dominated a row
of buildings in the first tier above the square. From there,
more rows of homes and shops climbed in irregular steps
up the steep hillside. Cobbled streets linked them all.
Townspeople claimed they had strong, shapely legs from
the constant climbing. Simone, carrying the baby, and
Lily, toting the luggage, made their way across the main
plaza and climbed to the boarding house. Madame
Lawrence herself opened the door to their red faces,
flushed from the climb. She greeted them with a wide,
gap-toothed smile, her broad face framed by salt and
pepper curls. Short and plump, she radiated welcome.
Simone sank into a waiting armchair and began shaking
with fatigue and relief. She looked down at the sleeping
baby in her arms and whispered, "For now, *ma petite*,
you are safe."

CHAPTER 4

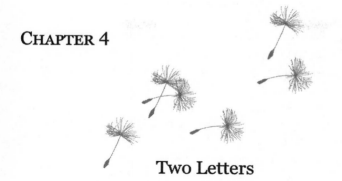

Two Letters

2 October 1940
Topeka, Kansas

Dearest Daniel,

Well, our little Maggie is nearly one. She is bright as a new penny. She says "Mama" for me and "Mimi" for grandma and "Dada" when we show her your picture. She seems to add a new word every day. Jacob keeps trying to get her to say his name, but she just laughs and claps her hands. She is not walking yet, but pulls up to the kitchen chairs and pushes them around.

We are all well at present. Your mother had a terrible cold this spring, but Doc Underwood made a couple of house calls and set her right in no time. And of course Berta's chicken soup can cure anything.

Berta and Jacob are such great help in the store, and tending Maggie, too. Maggie loves to bounce on Jacob's knee as he plays patty-cake and this-little-piggy with her. No matter how cranky she gets when she is tired or teething, she always grins and giggles when he smiles at her. She is truly a beautiful child. She has your eyes. (But, thank God, not your nose.) Her hair is dark and curly like your dad's and she has your mother's fair complexion. If she were not such a sweet baby, I'm afraid she would be spoiled beyond hope by the four of us.

Everywhere there is talk of war. The Isolationists continue to sway the President to keep out of it, saying it is Europe's problem. But more and more folks coming into the store seem to think Hitler will not stop until he forces America into the mess.

We have received a letter from Jacob's brother, Lev. Conditions in Germany are horrible for Jews; laws have been passed denying them property rights, jobs, forcing them into ghettos, even deporting them into labor camps. Anyone who stands up for them is jailed or worse. Lev and his family have managed to escape to France, but conditions are not much better there. So many refugees from fighting in Belgium and Poland crowd the cities that food is scarce and expensive, and the French are losing patience. German propaganda is convincing them that the Jews and other refugees are the cause of all their problems.

We all send our love and prayers for your safety. I pray that you will take care. I know you will be brave. I think of you every minute of every day and long to hear your voice telling me how much you love us. I'm sending along more cookies. Know they were made with love.

Hugs and Kisses, Ida

When the USA entered the war on December 7, 1941, Maggie Hagelman was two-and-a-half-years-old. She and her mother had not heard directly from her father, Daniel, for over eighteen months. Occasionally they would receive a cryptic, formal note from the British Royal Airforce that he was well and serving in a classified capacity. They continued to write to him regularly, but assumed their letters were in a file somewhere in London, waiting for him to return to his base. Maggie had a framed picture of him on the dresser by her little bed, and she kissed it every night before going to sleep. Cousins Jacob and Berta, Grandma, and Momma lavished her with love.

When President Roosevelt declared war on the Axis powers, the family prayed that the war's end was near. One day, Ida was helping Mrs. Hooley pay her monthly tab at the cash register, a process which always took time and patience as she fumbled in a little black purse for the exact change. Ida overheard a pair of upstanding neighborhood leaders discussing the war. One said to the other, "If we can make this war last a couple more years, I'll have it made for life."

Ida reached across the counter, grabbed the man by his tie, and jerked his face within a few inches of her own. "You stupid jackass!" she shouted into his startled face. "I'm willing to bet you sat out the last war and do not have a son risking his life in this one. My husband has been serving for eighteen months on classified missions in Europe. My little girl there knows him only from a photo. How dare you wish to extend this war for a single minute. Get out of our store, and never come back!"

"Not come back!" echoed Maggie, stamping her foot. "For shame!" added Mrs. Hooley.

That afternoon a curt message arrived from the officials in London. "We regret to inform you that Airman Daniel Hagelman is missing in action in southern France."

That same evening a radio newscaster quoted England's Prime Minister, Winston Churchill. "Americans always do the right thing, after they've tried everything else."

"Amen," added Cousin Jacob.

Two days later, a letter came.

23 February 1941

My Loves, I hope this letter will answer many of your questions. After I write it, I will seal it in an envelope, put it in a larger envelope, and address it. Then, to avoid the censors, I'm giving it to Lieutenant George Cunningham, who is going to see his parents in Yorkshire this weekend. His mother will post it for him. You can send your letters and packages to me through her return address. I hope this works.

I am proud to tell you that I have been named the leader of our crew. This means my superiors have confidence that I have mastered every aspect of our training: physical, emotional, intellectual.

In all honesty, I am a very good commando, but I must admit I am not the best. I have met the best and he is my friend. He is a young French aristocrat who excels in every aspect of our training and was named to take the training by the highest-ranking leadership of the French Resistance. He has already returned to France. I am sure we will meet again.

Our unit has been working especially hard training for a difficult mission. I cannot be specific about it because we won't know details until we begin. PM Churchill himself has approved the mission.. You might not recognize me with my bushy moustache and bulging muscles. I can now climb ropes, scale walls, and run 5 miles at a pretty brisk pace with a 50 lb. pack. I have also been working on learning a little French and some German. When I return to you, I will be a svelte, sophisticated man of the world.

Thank you from all of us for the package. The blokes cannot stop talking about the peanut butter cookies. Please send the recipe in your next letter (or package with more cookies.) I am so grateful also for the snapshots you sent. The shot of all of you in front of the store is pinned above my bunk. I touch it every night before I go to sleep. The picture of darling little Maggie with the lock of her hair is in a small wallet I carry next to my heart in my uniform pocket. I will never be without it. I love it that you added Daniella as her middle name. I will always be part of her, and I will always strive to live up to that honor.

I am now a glider pilot and part of an elite commando unit (Special Operations Executive or SOE) that includes mostly Brits, but a few Yanks and Canadians. The young Frenchman training with us, my friend, is named André Jabot. I am certainly glad he is on our side. I have never met a more intense, focused fellow. He will be a lethal force against the enemy. We are all volunteers, and among us are three women.

As a glider pilot, I become infantry as soon as the wheels touch the ground. Our missions are secret and dangerous and require stealth and flexibility; we must think on the go and deal with life-threatening obstacles as they arise. Our unit includes munitions experts, snipers, and wireless operators, and all of us are trained in hand-to-hand combat. Keep this close. This is secret information.

All this means that our loved ones must know that our survival rate is pretty low. My absence from you now is good training for what may come. I find comfort, Ida, that you and Maggie are safe with a good living, comfortable home, and family and friends around you to support and love you. My prayer is that our country will continue to grow as a land of freedom and acceptance, and that a despot such as Adolf Hitler never, never grows among our people. I also know what a strong, self-sufficient person you are. I hate it that the state of the world has brought us to this, but I cannot stand by and do nothing. I am compelled to fight, to resist, to die if necessary, to stop this evil. I love you more than life and beyond death.   Love, Daniel

Part II

Resistance

The Cross of Lorraine, or liberation cross, was the symbol of the Free French Forces in response to the German Nazi occupation. Though historically it appears as early as the 12th century, it was taken up by the Resistance as a rallying symbol for the recovery of French independence.

CHAPTER 1
Daniel and André

The First Missions

D aniel and his mates found the flight from the coast of Britain to the Haute Loire to be one bumpy, noisy ride. Conversation was almost impossible, and to bum a smoke, Daniel had to cup his hands and shout directly into Bertie's ear. The only light came from a sliver of moon, billions of stars, the flare of matches, and the glowing tips of cigarettes. The flight path stretched south from Dover, low over the English Channel, then headed inland over the coast of Brittany to avoid detection by ground-based anti-aircraft guns. For three hours, Daniel and his group of saboteurs sat on hard wooden benches and endured the deafening roar of the engines. Jumping into the black night and parachuting into the unknown below would be a relief from the incessant noise.

In the air, the pilot received coded instructions by wireless from a Resistance operator on the ground with coordinates for the drop. André Jabot and his *Résistants* would be in place at the selected site to signal the pilot with code blinked from a flashlight. The co-pilot would flash an answer that the code had been received. The reception crew would then scatter to define the drop zone with their flashlights.

As soon as each parachutist touched ground, he or she began to shed the chute, roll it into a tight wad, and bury it with the help of the reception crew. Together they located all the equipment also dropped by parachute: long carefully packed canisters filled with food, weapons, ammunition, wireless equipment, clothing, counterfeit francs, and explosives. Every piece had to be found, every canister accounted for, to avoid detection by the enemy. They certainly did not want to face German soldiers shooting at them with their own guns and ammunition.

SOE agents and Resistance fighters would then assist and guide the unit to a safe house. From there, they divided into smaller units, each with a specific assignment: a bridge to blow up, a troop train to wreck, an important Nazi officer to assassinate, or a wireless center to install. Wireless communication was indispensable. The Germans were adept at locating radio transmissions and the wireless operators were the most hunted and most frequently captured of all saboteurs. Capture meant certain torture and death.

Daniel's crew included Alice Upstill, an expert wireless operator. Petite Alice astounded her male SOE classmates and their trainers by being the fastest rope climber, finishing third in a cross-country run, and besting a six-foot, 200-pound former boxer in hand-to-hand combat. With her long blond hair in braids and her small frame, she looked like someone's little sister, which worked well as a built-in disguise.

The third member of their unit, Bertie MacIntosh, their Scottish explosives whiz, owned a temper that matched his job and his violently red beard. For luck, Bertie insisted on wearing a kilt to start every mission.

Daniel joked that he was glad they always jumped in the dark, but just to be safe, he insisted on jumping from the plane *after* Bertie. Bertie was a traditionalist; he wore his kilt sans underwear, in true commando style. The ground crew was led by their Resistance guide, fellow SOE graduate, André Jabot.

Daniel and André made a quick, happy reunion. Gripping hands and thumping each other on the back, even kissing cheeks in the French manner. "After we blow up this train and send some Germans to hell, we will drink some wine and have a delicious meal back in Lyon," said André .

"Which is the best restaurant in Lyon?" Daniel asked.

"All French restaurants are excellent. And in Lyon there are many. To find a good one, just toss a rock," André answered.

On this particular mission, their crew was to wire and blow a section of railroad track just north of Lyon. Wrecking the tracks and derailing a passing train would create a tangle of track and train cars that would disrupt German troop movements for weeks. They would be traveling on foot from the drop zone to Lyon, a distance of about 100 kilometers. The trip would take three days through densely forested hills, avoiding paved roads and villages. They would spend daylight hours resting in homes and barns of families sympathetic to the Resistance and walk country roads and trails through the trees at night, taking care to avoid any German checkpoints.

On the second night of the journey, as they walked steadily on a narrow path through the trees single file, they happened onto a German soldier relieving himself on a pine tree. Fortunately André was leading the line and the soldier was not armed. They were both surprised, but the soldier made the mistake of taking time to tuck up. André dispatched him with a quick slash to the throat. A German sentry shouted, "Wer geht dahin?" (Who goes there?)

André answered in perfect German, "Ein Bär pisst in den Wald." (A bear pissing in the woods.) They waited quietly for half an hour, then went back to a fork in the trail and took the other path, shorter but steeper, leading also to the rendezvous point a few miles north of Lyon. They would meet three more Resistance fighters who would help provide surveillance while they placed their explosives, wiring, and detonators.

The team reached the site mid-afternoon on the third day as planned. Their Resistance crew was there waiting for them. André knew all three and quickly made introductions. The Frenchmen took up positions on the embankments on either side of the railway. Daniel, Bertie, and Alice busied themselves setting the charges, with Bertie giving orders about placements and connections. Explosives were arranged so that the low hanging tender would catch a trip wire after the engine had passed. This would ensure that both the engine and tender would be destroyed, and the rest of the cars would pile up and spill down the embankment, mangling a long section of rail and crossties.

"According to the schedule, the train we're targeting will be passing just at dusk. This will give us time to leave the scene and head to the hideout in the forest under cover of darkness," André said as he checked his watch.

The train was ten minutes late. It was travelling at about 45 kph when it hit the trip wire. The explosion lifted both the engine and tender from the tracks and the wooden freight cars piled up behind them, zigzagging like a fractured snake. The first three cars burst into flames from the explosives. The fourth car began to burn and then exploded with a tremendous blast that sent a shock wave into the surrounding forest. The commandos were knocked off their feet even though they were standing two hundred yards away.

"Holy Shite!" Bertie bellowed as he leapt to his feet. Daniel and Alice slowly stood and watched, awestruck. Any tree within fifty yards of the blast flared and sent plumes of dense smoke into the sky. More cars exploded with similar force. They had accomplished more than disrupting troop transportation. By merest chance, they had blown up a whole train loaded with barrels of gasoline headed north to fuel German Panzers and troop carriers. "I dunna think Adolf will be 'appy," Bertie observed.

Later, André and his Resistance team led the crew several miles through the dense trees to a secluded cabin stocked with food and clothing appropriate for the next part of their mission to Lyon. "Our organizers at SOE pay careful attention to detail," observed Alice. "They took no chance that we might be spotted by wearing clothes that might draw attention by being too new or too foreign. Look, they even sent used shoes in the airdrops to match the clothing for each of us."

The team washed in a stream of cold snowmelt from the mountains and wrapped themselves into wool blankets as the Frenchmen warmed some canned stew over a small fire behind the cabin. After a brisk rubdown, they dressed and ate stew, crusty bread, and cheese. Daniel remembered his mother telling him, "Hunger is the best spice." They would sleep in their clothes on pallets on the plank floor. Daniel thought to himself, "And exhaustion is a soft mattress."

Outside, under a pine-covered tarp, waited a dilapidated truck loaded with cabbages. The next morning, the SOE team hid in the bed among the cabbages, and André drove them into Lyon to a restaurant in Old Town where they crawled from the cabbages and stepped into a passageway leading to a safe house.

Old Lyon had sprouted, like most human settlements, because of the presence of a river, or in the case of Lyon, two rivers. The town had grown on a long peninsula between the Rhône and Saône Rivers where they joined to become the mighty Rhône as it continued south to the Mediterranean Sea. A warren of gray granite buildings and cobbled streets filled all available land. Some of the ancient buildings rose three stories high. From the street, many were accessible only by doors in the walls formed as one building butted directly against the next. The doors were locked to all but those living in the homes or operating first floor street-side businesses, and keys were given only to close, trusted family and friends. Stepping inside the door was like stepping into another world.

As he stepped through the doorway, Daniel noted an immediate change in atmosphere. Breezes from the rivers died, and the air became cool and quiet, scented by the honeysuckle vines climbing sunward. The garish reds, oranges, and greens from beyond the door faded to soft, shaded pastels, as the sun penetrated directly only at midday. At first, the damp stillness seemed to press in upon them, but several meters inside, the narrow alley widened into a courtyard separating homes rising above it on either side. Some presented a small patio trimmed with potted hosta and perhaps a bench or two. On one, hydrangea vines with trunks like trees wound their way up stone columns to the roofline. A burbling fountain provided drinks for the pigeons and soothing background sound for anyone resting on a bench or enjoying a coffee behind an open window. Some of the buildings featured narrow turrets housing spiral stairs which conveyed residents to the upper stories.

These passages gave a feeling of shelter, cool solitude, privacy, and safety from all the bustle beyond that secret door. Daniel imagined Ida, up high on one of the balconies above, calling down to him, like Juliet to her Romeo. André explained, "These passages are called *traboules*. They serve as alleyways between streets." Daniel found the passage to be the perfect path to a hidden sanctuary for his group of exhausted, hunted spies.

Lyon, the second largest city in France, was a beehive of subversive activity. A city of commerce, education, culture, and fierce independence, Lyon offered support for the Resistance and tolerance for British spies. In spite of this support, Daniel and his team had to be extremely careful. Some of that humming in the hive came from German agents and counter agents.

Klaus Barbie, a leader of Hitler's personal bodyguard known as the SS and like all members of the SS, a dedicated Jew hunter, operated a prison and torture center in the *Hôtel Terminus* near the train station. He became known as "The Butcher of Lyon" for his lust for torture and death. As a result, codes were altered frequently, identities camouflaged, and aliases changed often. And some agents were masters of disguise. Daniel's guide and elusive SOE agent, André Jabot, dressed as a schoolgirl, had once escaped capture by walking meekly past a party of German officers.

One of Daniel's duties was to requisition supplies from the British using coded messages transmitted by wireless. The most important supply came in the form of millions in counterfeit French francs, handy for bribing Vichy officials and purchasing rationed food and medicine on the black market.

Wily, ruthless, and a born organizer, Daniel's friend André soon became a high priority target for the Nazis. Multiple identities and constant movement made him a shadowy presence, elusive and undefinable. He soon became known by his *nom de le guerre: L'ombre,* The Shadow.

It was important that no agent draw attention or arouse suspicion. Even so, many were caught, tortured, and killed. SOE agents routinely carried cyanide tablets in case of capture, especially if they had knowledge vital to the cause that could be tortured out of them. Biting down on a tablet hidden in a hollow tooth would quickly produce a gasping, strangling, death.

Daniel, Bertie, Alice, and André hurried to carry all their gear up one of the turret staircases to a small room on the top floor. Below them a two-bedroom apartment occupied by the Rousset family, owners of *Le*

Lyon, a sidewalk cafe on the street below. The Roussets were active members and supporters of the Resistance. By nightfall, the wireless was set up and ready to send messages. To help avoid detection by German search teams, their equipment included a battery and mechanical generator which could be attached to a stationary bicycle provided by the local Resistance team. This made their unit portable and harder to detect as it was not plugged into an outlet. Surges in use of electricity might arouse suspicion. Bertie would study maps, pedal the generator, and keep fit all at the same time. Alice observed, "I wish he'd buried that damn kilt with his parachute!" The following morning coded messages arrived, outlining their next assignment.

CHAPTER 2
Simone

A New Life in Le Chambon

The people of Le Chambon were skilled in the art of helping refugees blend into new lives in their midst. History had taught them the trauma of persecution and the upset of new surroundings and new people. They understood the healing power of time and love.

Simone slept well. When she awoke, it took her a few seconds to remember where she was. Her room with Madame Lawrence was on the second floor of the boarding house. A window near her bed presented a view of the plaza below: the winding river Lignon flanked by a grassy park and a backdrop of forested mountains; she could not believe that just two days before, she had left her parents and her home in Paris. Those familiar tears began to sting behind her eyes. Suddenly she remembered Marie. She turned to find an empty pallet. She hurried into the hall and looked down from the stair rail to the foyer below. She heard spoons tinkling on coffee cups coming from the dining room, and the murmur of voices. Simone hurried to brush her teeth, comb her hair, splash water on her face, dress, and clip down the wooden staircase.

In the dining room, a ring of smiling faces greeted her. Lily sat at one end of the long table cuddling Marie, who was guzzling a bottle of condensed milk. Madame Lawrence stepped into the room from the kitchen with a bowl of boiled eggs and a basket of brioche. Already a carafe of hot coffee and pots of fruit jam sat next to a plate of sliced cheeses. "*Bon appétit, ma chere*," she said. "You slept well?"

"*Oui, merci*," Simone replied. "I was a little confused when I first awoke and concerned to find an empty pallet, but here you all are, and here are Lily and Marie content and safe. It is comforting to see all your friendly faces."

"Sit and eat while we plan your first day in Le Chambon," Lily suggested. "I think we should visit the school and introduce you to the students. We can then walk around the square and you can get to know some of the shopkeepers and their businesses. We can have lunch at *Le Petite Table*, take a stroll through the park, then return to rescue Madame Lawrence from Marie and put her down for a nap. I think a nap would be good for both of us as well."

Simone smiled, "It seems to me you have planned a perfect tour to acquaint me with the village and its people. This will be a great beginning of my new life. Now, please introduce me to these smiling faces."

Lily smiled. "Of course," she said. "Here on my right are the LeMondes, George and Evelyn. They both teach history at the *Université*. Next to them is Henri Longet, Madame Lawrence's handyman. If you have a dripping faucet or loose floorboard, he is the one to fix it. This pretty lady at the end is *Mam'selle* Janine Phillipe who teaches Spanish at the *Université*. On my left are Suzette and Louis Manet. They manage the gardens and grounds, and help with housekeeping and cooking."

Just then the front door opened and there was a great clattering in the hall. In bounded twins Marshall and Oliver Pavin followed by their mother, Annette.

"*Maman* Lala," they shouted. "We are here!" they announced in perfect unison.

Lily began laughing. Marie flung out her arms, squinted her eyes, made a face consuming O with her mouth, and screamed.

"Obviously the twins have arrived," Simone observed. The boys calmed to a simmer and stepped up to introduce themselves to Simone and Marie, who quieted and took them in with serious concentration. Baby Marie seemed to decide they were not a threat and gave them a wide-eyed smile. Annette introduced herself to Simone, pulled up a chair and helped herself to a coffee.

Madame Lawrence gave the boys a long double hug. No one need ever ask if they were identical. Alike as two pennies and always dressed to match, they often spoke in unison and sometimes finished each other's sentences. Lala, as the boys called her, told them, "This is Baby Marie. She has come to join our little nursery school. You will be big brothers to her and help her to grow and learn. You must not be wild things around her because she is tiny, and loud noises frighten little ones. Do you understand?" Marshall and Oliver nodded solemnly in unison.

Lily passed the baby to Lala and said to Simone, "Let's begin our tour."

By the end of the week, Simone had begun working with the students at the elementary school. Some of the students were from the village and others were from refugee families. Some, like Simone, were sent by their parents to escape the Nazi threat in Paris. Many of them had been taken in by families from Le Chambon and the surrounding countryside. Simone helped with their studies, but her chief interest lay in teaching perspective, composition, and drawing. She was convinced that artistic expression was as good an outlet for them as it was for her. Some of the images they created were powerful portrayals of fear and horror. She found that getting these images onto paper seemed to unburden their minds and hearts. As time passed, the students created less oppressive images.

One of her favorite students, twelve-year-old Colette, began to sketch landscapes full of trees and mountains instead of haunting, hollow-eyed faces. One day as Colette was working on a charcoal sketch, Simone asked her, "What has changed, Colette? Why have you stopped sketching those scary faces?"

"You know, *Maîtresse*, I am not really sure. Those faces have haunted me since the SS came to our home in Lyon to question my father about his silk business. Our family owned a silk mill, several workhouses with huge three-story looms, and a shop which sold finished silk by the yard. We employed almost a hundred workers. The officer wanted to know if any of his workers were Jews. My father told the man he did not inquire about such personal things as religion. The officer hit my father right in the face with the butt of his pistol and broke his nose. The two Vichy policemen with him took my parents for questioning. I have not seen or heard from them since. My mother was six months pregnant. My nanny, Anne Amore, grew up here in Le Chambon. She brought me here. The faces that I draw come to me in my dreams. I think they come from the hate I saw in that German officer's cold blue eyes as he hit my Papa. Since you have begun teaching us, the faces are fading. I do not dream of them so often."

"I have begun to notice this place and to see changes in the faces of the other children here. My little friend Levi, the dark-haired boy who seldom speaks, came from a holding camp near the town of Gurs not far from the border with Spain. He was put into the camp along with his mother and grandmother because they are Jews. Conditions there were horrible. The huts where they stayed had no heat, no beds, no windows. There was hardly any food. His grandmother fell ill and died. His mother tried to take him and escape and was shot to death by the guards. At last, a group of young nurses came from the Red Cross. Levi was so small and thin that one of the nurses was able to smuggle him out in a basket of laundry. She brought him here where she heard he would be safe. Bless you, *Maîtresse* Simone, for showing us this new way of noticing the world."

Simone added a drawing of Colette working on one of her own sketches to her diary. She also helped Colette and Levi and the others begin collecting their work in personal portfolios. In the back of her mind, she began to see a path for herself, these children, and the art they were creating. She imagined a way forward, to what their world might become after the war. She dreamed of a school, a boarding school, where children scarred by war could find love, success, and a reason to live. Whenever she dreamed of this school, she recalled the lovely pink house on the riverbank near Vienne.

Colette at Work

After several months, Lily asked Simone if she would be willing to perform a useful and relatively safe task for the Resistance. Her job would be to move food to a Resistance stronghold at the foot of the mountains about an hour's bicycle ride to the north. She would travel by bicycle with panniers filled with bread, vegetables, and fruit. Simone agreed and began making the journey two or three days a week after school. After several uneventful trips, she was surprised one afternoon to find a Vichy police checkpoint just a few miles from Le Chambon.

Two fresh-faced young Vichy officers ordered her to halt. "Your papers?" one asked. She retrieved the documents from the pouch inside her jacket. "Where are you going, Simone Bouret?"

"I am delivering produce from my landlady. She trades vegetables from her garden and bread from her ovens to Jacques Gaston, a woodchopper who lives in the forest of the foothills. In return, he provides the boarding house with firewood," Simone explained. "Would you both like an apple, or perhaps one of Madame's delicious brioche?"

"Both would be excellent." She complied, and they waved her on down the road. She completed her delivery as usual. The guards waved her through without incident or comment on the way back. On her next trip, a routine was established. They accepted the food and no longer checked her papers. They began to greet her with smiles. One observed to the other, "The rolls are delicious, and so is she."

At breakfast one morning, Lily asked Simone, "Would you mind making your delivery a bit more risky?"

"Please explain," Simone responded.

"We have received ammunition and explosives from an air drop recently. They could be packed into your panniers under the food. Are you willing to face the added danger? If you are caught, you would be tortured and shot. We would provide you with a small poison tablet that would provide a gentler death."

"*Oui*, I will do it," she answered without hesitation.

On her first trip through the checkpoint after the munitions were added under the vegetables and bread, she was surprised to see a German soldier there with the two Vichy policemen. She approached calmly and glided her bike to a stop. The German demanded her papers and scanned them thoroughly, then asked, "Where exactly are you going, Madamoiselle Bouret?"

"As these officers know, I go twice every week to deliver food to Jacques Gaston, a forester in the foothills, from Madame Lawrence, my landlady. She raises fruit and vegetables, but Jacques especially enjoys her brioche. In return he supplies wood during the winter for the fireplaces at her boarding house. These two officers will testify that the quality of her produce is excellent," she said quietly.

"Yes, Sergeant," one of the Vichy guards added, "the brioche is delicious. I'm sure she can spare two or three."

"As you wish. We will have three," the German answered. Simone stepped from her bike and handed the German officer the rolls. He waved her on, then ate them all.

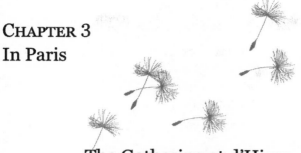

CHAPTER 3
In Paris

The Gathering at d'Hiver

In the early morning of July 16, 1942, the moment came that Rachel's (Simone's) parents had long dreaded: a pounding at their front door. Ben opened the door to find three armed Paris policemen who demanded that all members of the household were to accompany them. Each member of each targeted household had ten minutes to gather two shirts, a sweater, a pair of shoes, and a blanket. They would be attending a meeting at an unnamed gathering place. Esther also grabbed two loaves of bread and a bottle of wine which she rolled into her blanket. Ben tucked a small bottle of pills into the inside pocket of his jacket. They joined a group of others from the neighborhood and began walking toward the Eiffel Tower, not far from their home. They noticed that everyone in the group wore the yellow star the Nazis forced upon them to identify themselves as Jews. As they walked, truckloads of others under police guard passed them, headed in the same direction.

Their destination was the Vélodrome d'Hiver located near The Eiffel Tower. The building was a cycling track and special event venue for boxing, fencing, and cycling. Families gathered in groups on the grassy areas around the arena. A small group of Jews from nearby who had been escorted by police sat on the grass waiting to see what this "*rafle*" was all about and watching their small children at play. Two three-year-olds were picking and scattering dandelion seed heads, giggling as they filled their cheeks and puffed the seeds into the wind. Just as toddler Paul handed his friend Annette a ball of fluff on a stem, policemen descended upon the group. They began separating all children under fifteen years of age from their families. Babies and toddlers were ripped screaming from the arms of their parents. One of the officers grabbed Paul and Annette as other officers restrained the parents with clubs and guns. Lifting the toddlers by their arms, he dropped them into the bed of a truck. Paul howled and kicked his attacker in the face as he was lifted above the side of the truck. Annette's screams, "*MAMAN, MAMAN!*" echoed down the streets and through the neighborhood.

Older children saw and understood what was happening. Those who tried to run were shot. Mothers and fathers who refused to let their children go were clubbed into submission or unconsciousness. The children, including Paul and Annette, were ultimately taken east to the death camps. Those who survived the journey by cattle car were gassed upon arrival, and their tiny lifeless bodies were heaved into the cremation ovens.

By noon the sports venue was packed full of Jews. The d'Hiver's glass roof was painted dark blue to mask it from Allied bombers. All the doors and windows were sealed, and the temperature soon rose alarmingly. For five days, 13,152 Jews were sealed in hell with no lavatories, little food, and only one tap for water. Those who tried to escape were shot. Some committed suicide.

Rachel's parents, Ben and Esther Ropfogel, were among those who died, aided by Ben's little bottle of cyanide tablets. After five days, those who remained alive were loaded into cattle cars and taken east. The few who survived the journey went to Auschwitz.

And later, when crews came to clean the offal from the Vélodrome, on the wide sidewalk in front of the entrance, the dried stems of Annette and Paul's dandelions were trampled beneath their boots and scattered by a hot, merciless wind.

Most of those in charge of the *Vel d'Hiver* roundup were fellow Frenchmen. The Nazis were especially casual in dealing death to the old, to the children, and to the infirm; all these were useless to them as slaves. The gas chambers of death camps like Auschwitz were the cheapest, most efficient way to dispose of them.

Years later Rachel's adopted daughter Marie found Benjamin and Esther Ropfogel's names on the list of those imprisoned by the *rafle of d'Hiver*; this information would end years of searching. Marie was sure that Rachel's mother and father, her adoptive grandparents, were dead, but like countless other survivors, she would never know exactly when or how Rachel's people had perished. The same was true of Marie's birth parents and her two brothers.

Chapter 4

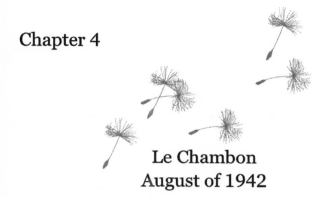

Le Chambon
August of 1942

Rachel had lived as Simone Bouret in Le Chambon for over two years. The pattern of life for her and Baby Marie had settled into a comfortable routine. She dressed Marie each morning and fed her breakfast as she ate her own. She then left for the school and Marie spent the day with Lala and the twins. Twice a week in the late afternoon Simone made her deliveries.

Marie began tottering to outstretched arms and could say "Lala," "Mama," and wave goodbye. The twins introduced her to "*non.*" All three wilted to the floor, dissolving into peals of laughter whenever she frowned, shook her finger, stomped her foot, and said perfectly, "*Non, non, non!*" She continued to be a happy child with a ready smile. The boys loved to find ways to make her laugh. They all played choo-choo by lining up apple crates and pushing them around the dining room. Lala read to them every day and the boys were beginning to read some of the simpler stories to Marie. Simone was not sure if they were reading or simply had memorized all the words. Either way, Marie was delighted with the attention.

As the Resistance grew and became more destructive, the German authorities reinforced the checkpoint on

Simone's route and began posting additional checkpoints in other locations. Simone continued to make her deliveries. She had almost become part of the scenery. Now, however, she delivered a dozen brioche for the officers, who smiled and waved when they saw her coming. As the guards became more and more accustomed to her comings and goings, she carried more and more pistols, ammunition, plastic explosive, fuses, and wiring in her panniers, and fewer and fewer carrots and apples.

Simone was constantly amazed by the German soldiers who sometimes came to Le Chambon in summer to relax and recuperate in the cool mountain air. The hotel where most of them stayed was just across the street from the school where many of the refugee children lived and studied. It seemed so odd to her that none of the Germans ever questioned, or even seemed to notice, how many children crowded the village. Why did these Germans with their precise minds, who made countless lists and totaled rows and rows of numbers, not see the imbalance between adults and children in this isolated little town?

In Lyon
Orders by Wireless

SOE wireless operator Alice Upstill sat in the hideaway in Lyon wearing her cumbersome headphones, translating dots and dashes into letters as they came in. The next step was to decode the resulting words and phrases. All SOE agents studied Morse code, but Alice was a master at speed and accuracy. Agents would also listen to BBC Radio broadcasts from England as they ended each night with "personal announcements." These often included coded messages which might give agents information about German troop movements or planned Allied attacks. Just as often these messages were a jumble of nonsense words to keep German interceptors off balance.

At four o'clock one morning the wireless began clicking. Alice quickly shook off sleep, donned her headphones, and began transcribing. The entire process took about twenty minutes. The message outlined a sizeable operation involving several truckloads of German troops. Daniel, Bertie, and André Jabot and his forty-five Resistance fighters, would travel by truck toward the village of Le Chambon-sur-Lignon. Alice would stay behind to continue communications with headquarters in Britain.

In spring, beekeepers traditionally trucked loads of hives to the lavender fields and orchards to pollinate the flowers. One such truck would be modified to carry

Resistance fighters into an ambush of German troops being transported into the Haught Loire region to strengthen German control there. This truck was loaded on sides, back, and top with beehives. Fighters would crowd into a hollow space in the center of the arrangement of hives. The hives at the rear of the truck were mounted on a cleverly-constructed, swinging tailgate that would allow the fighters to unload and take positions on both sides of the road, where they would lie in wait for the troop carriers. The operation was to take place the following day.

In Le Chambon
Following the Mission

One night, just before dawn when the dark is darkest, there came a coded tap at the kitchen door of Madame Lawrence's boarding house. Madame Lawrence opened the door to André Jabot, one of his men, and an injured British saboteur. "This man is one of us," Jabot explained. "He was wounded when he and our SOE team and a company of Resistance fighters ambushed two German personnel carriers bringing soldiers to Le Chambon to strengthen German control in this area. We have carried him for almost three miles. He has two bullets in his right leg, a wound on his neck, and he is unconscious, probably from loss of blood."

The Germans had all been killed. Lala sent Louis the gardener to fetch the doctor.

Then she and Suzette made up the bed in a hidden room behind a chifforobe in Simone's room on the second floor. Even when the furniture was moved away, the entrance to the room was cleverly disguised by the paneling. Lala then hurried to the kitchen to make tea and coffee. She also boiled some eggs, sliced a ham, and filled a basket with yesterday's brioche.

Simone sat with the two *Résistants* as they ate. "Who are you?" she asked André. She noticed his aristocratic manner of speaking and refined bearing. "My name is André Jabot. My family lives near Soissons. My little brother was killed when the Nazis blitzed our area to force the treasonous surrender of France by the Vichy traitors."

"Are you related to Charlotte Jabot?" Simone asked. "My mother is Esther Ropfogel. She is a portrait painter in Paris. I am sure Charlotte's husband, Jean-Claude, commissioned my mother to paint a portrait of her."

"Yes, they are my mother and father," André answered. "Just imagine the chance that fate brings us together in this remote place! Your mother is indeed a gifted artist. She captured my mother's distinctive features and the fire of her character. The portrait hangs in our hall. Unfortunately, it is now admired by German officers who occupy our home. I pray that she and my brothers are still well in the half of the house the Germans so generously share with my family. If that detestable pack of vermin has any sense, they will realize that their reign of terror is at an end, do no further harm to my family, and retreat before *la Résistance* and the Allies come to rout them. If I catch them there, I will show no more mercy than they gave my little brother." After a pause to let his anger subside, he asked, "How is it that you are here?"

Simone understood his anger, but was awed by its intensity. After a pause, she answered, "My father, Benjamin Ropfogel, is a banker in Paris. We are Jews. As the Germans made clear their hatred of us, my parents sent me here to Le Chambon to be safe until the war is over. I used to be their daughter Rachel. Now I am Simone Bouret. I, too, am with the *la Résistance*. I have been here for four years. I have not heard a word from my parents in all that time. I don't know if they are alive or dead. Sometimes I struggle to remember their faces, but then they come to me in my dreams, and I am home in my room and hear my mother calling for me to come to breakfast. In my diary, I also have a sketch of them waving goodbye from the front steps. I miss my old life, my old self." Suddenly the pain fell upon her. All the pent -up fear, and anger, and long-suppressed tears burst from her heart.

André moved his chair next to her and circled her with his arms. He let her cry until the storm subsided. Finally he lifted her chin, pushed a curl from her forehead, and wiped away the tears. "You have been as brave as any *saboteur*, but the worst is yet to come. You must rebuild the walls and return to being Simone Bouret, fearless *Résistant*. If we make it alive through the end of this war, I will find you. Perhaps together we can help find peace. Now you must help my friend, Daniel.

He is a brave member of *la Résistance*, an American volunteer with the British. I would bet my life that he will recover and return to the fight."

Simone called to Suzette to make up a room upstairs for the Frenchmen, but after they had eaten and accepted a parcel of more food, they insisted on leaving. "One man is easier to hide than three," André observed. "Our presence here endangers all of you. Besides, we must return to our business of ridding our country of this dreadful German pestilence."

Doctor Mason came quietly to the back door. He brought sterilized instruments, bandages, antibiotics, and ether. He instructed Simone on how to hold the gauze above the patient's nose to administer the anesthetic, cleaned all three wounds with iodine, and removed the bullets. The neck wound was just a graze and required no stitches. "Will he live?" asked Simone.

"If he has not lost too much blood, and if I have enough antibiotics to hold off infection, he probably has a good chance. If the Germans find him, all of us will die."

CHAPTER 5

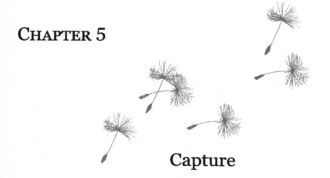

Capture

Later that morning as the two, André and his friend, slipped along a narrow forest path north of Le Chambon, they ran into a German patrol. Caught in a crossfire of swarming bullets, they were both hit. André's companion took three bullets to the chest and died instantly. A bullet tore through André's shoulder and slammed him to the ground. Struggling to his feet, he began to run. A German soldier stepped from behind a tree as he passed and smashed the back of his head with the butt of his rifle. André fell to the ground, unconscious.

Afterward, the Germans began searching homes in the nearest village, looking for other stragglers from the ambush. They did not find the British agent. They did, however, arrest thirty random locals, men ranging in age from fifteen to eighty-four, line them up against the wall of the village church, and shoot them to death in retaliation for the soldiers killed in the ambush. Then they delivered their comatose captive to *Standardenführer* Fredrik Haught at *Hôtel Terminus*, dreaded SS headquarters, in Lyon.

Awakenings

That afternoon, as Simone prepared to burn the British agent's clothing, she noticed a small wallet in the breast pocket of his jacket. When she opened it, she discovered a worn photograph of a little girl about the same age as Marie. She wore a crisp summer dress. The photo caught her sitting quietly, looking away from the photographer into the distance. The similarity of the child to Marie was, in fact, remarkable. She seemed to radiate the same happy disposition. They could have been sisters. On the back of the photo was written in neat script, *Maggie Daniella Hagelman, age 3 1/2 years*, and taped there was a wispy curl of fine brown hair.

The Yank, as he became known to the household, was unconscious for three days. Doctor Mason came every day after his office hours, under the guise of buying bread for dinner in case anyone became suspicious. He found Simone to be a dependable nurse, following his instructions efficiently: wounds cleaned and dressed, IV saline and glucose drips administered twice daily, bedding and patient clean and tidy. As she tended him, she talked to him as if he were an old friend. "I found your photo of Maggie in your pocket. I hope you don't mind that I went through your clothes before burning them. Your little girl is so precious. I have a daughter, too, born the same year. In fact, they look so alike, almost twin sisters. Her name is Marie, Marie and Maggie. I would hope someday they could meet and grow to be friends. It must be so painful to be gone from her to this war. I feel this pain of separation as well. When you wake up, we will have long talks about missing those we love."

Later that morning as she was tucking in the bedcovers, she saw his left foot move a little. "Sir, Sir, can you hear me?" She picked up his hand. "Squeeze my fingers." There was a tiny pressure. "Open your eyes." A slight flicker, then his eyes opened. For the first time, she really looked into his face. His hazel eyes, pupils dilated, began to focus.

"Where am I?" he rasped. "Who are you? What has happened?"

"The doctor ordered this shot if you awakened. It is to control pain, but it will also help you rest. He says the next time you wake, you will be more alert, and the pain should lessen as you heal. I will answer all your questions tomorrow. And I will ask a few of my own."

André at *Hôtel Terminus*, House of Torture

Return to consciousness came for André with throbbing pain. His head seemed a lead weight impossible to lift. His shoulder burned. His body pressed into the rough, stone floor beneath him. Eyes opened to disorienting, absolute darkness. A nameless smell-fog of dried blood, feces, and acrid urine pierced his nostrils. Screams echoed from underground hallways. Consciousness fled.

André gasped awake as a bucket of icy water was dashed into his face. Before him stood a leering blue-eyed SS officer and two henchmen armed for torture. "Your name, please. Let's begin with your name," said officer Fredrik Haught.

André's SOE training was his only armor: *"When confronted with torture, anger is the best defense."* The adrenalin produced by anger would dull the pain of torture. "Where am I? Who are you? Why have you hurt me?" he shouted, shaking with rage.

"As you can see, I am an officer of the Führer's Third Reich, and you are an enemy spy who has killed many German soldiers. You are not in the uniform of the French Army; therefore, you have no rights as an enemy combatant. You are a lawless murderer. I intend to extract any information in any way I see fit, and then I will have you transported into the forest where you will dig your own grave. You will be shot in the legs and buried alive. Or we can forgo the torture. You can volunteer what you know. Then a quick shot to the temple will give you a painless end. Now, give me your name."

"After rage, use deflection." André's rage suddenly disappeared. He became confused and disoriented and began to drool and babble. "My name, yes, my name . . . what is my name? Why am I bleeding? My head hurts. My shoulder hurts. Where am I? Why can I not remember my name?"

At a nod from Haught, his men lifted André roughly and strapped him into a blood-stained wooden chair. One of them held his arm while the other tore the fingernails from his left hand. André's screams now joined the chorus echoing along the hallways of the *Hôtel Terminus.*

"Tell me your name!" Haught again demanded.

"I don't remember my name, you bastard!" André screamed.

"Take him away," Haught commanded his men. "Send someone to tend his wounds and give him food and water. Clean him up and let him rest. We must get him coherent enough to respond to questioning."

CHAPTER 6
Recovery

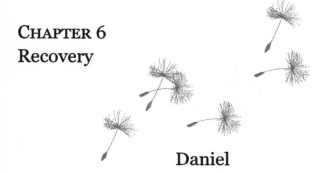

Daniel

The Yank wakened just before noon the day after being given the sedative. The tall girl was there. He remembered her from the day before; tall and slim, curly shoulder-length, dark hair, large expressive brown eyes.

"Tell me your name," he whispered. His throat was dry and sore.

"I am Simone Bouret," she answered. "I teach art to children in the school here."

"Where is here?"

"You are in Le Chambon-sur-Lignon, brought here by two fighters in *la Résistance*. There was an ambush of German troops north of the village several miles. The men who brought you said you are American."

"Right, American. Joined the British RAF to fight with the allies in '39—got tired of waiting for America to do something. With SOE, Churchill's commando force. Hurts to talk. My boots—where are my boots?"

"Under your bed. I cleaned them. I burned your clothes. The bullet holes would have given you away. I also found a wallet with a child's photo. It is here on the bedside table."

Daniel turned to look. As he took in his daughter's image, tears filled his eyes. Wiping away the tears, he turned to Simone. After a moment he said, "Now fill me in, please."

"Yes, of course, "Simone responded. You were brought here four nights ago by your friend André Jabot and one of his men. The local doctor has removed two bullets from your right leg and splinted the upper leg because one of the bullets cracked the femur. A bullet also grazed your neck, which may be the reason your voice is raspy. Any one of the wounds could have killed you. You are a lucky man. You are being well tended. There is healthy food and clean water here, and a good doctor with medicine to help you. Doctor Mason says it will take at least three months for the bone to heal enough to bear weight. At that point you can begin to rebuild the strength in your leg so that you will have full use of it. You must be patient and do as you are told to make a full recovery. Now, do you think you could drink a little broth and some water?"

He answered with a nod. "More sleep, too. And a bedpan. And my name is Daniel."

"Yes, I know," Simone responded. "Your friend André told me about you."

After waking later that same afternoon, Daniel sat on the edge of his bed and dangled his legs for a few minutes. Then with the help of Simone and Louis the handyman and a pair of crutches, he was able to stand and hobble around the room. In a week he could walk up and down the upstairs hallway, being careful always to bend his right knee so that his toes just brushed the floor. With the help of Louis he could use the bathroom at the end of the hall, shave, and wash himself. The staircase was of course an obstacle so, for the present, he remained upstairs. It was imperative that he stay within easy escape to the hidden room in the event of a Nazi search party.

One morning when Simone brought his breakfast, Daniel asked her to fetch a second cup so they could share the carafe of coffee on his tray. He also offered to share his chocolate brioche. "This is a bribe," he confessed. "I want to know more about you, where you come from, your family, why your English is better than mine."

"No need for bribery," Simone said with a smile. "I am from Paris. My parents sent me here to be safe from the Nazis. My English is good because my mother is American. My father's family have been bankers in Paris for four generations. We are Jews, and Simone Bouret is not my real name but, for now, that is who I have become. My mother is an artist and I share this passion with her. I teach art to the children of the primary school here in Le Chambon. There is more, but let's save the rest for another conversation—a chance for me to steal another brioche!"

"Thank you for sharing your story, Simone. My family came from Germany to America two generations ago, fleeing oppression. I am a Jew as well."

Madame Lawrence was delighted with Daniel's increasing appetite and provided him with three healthy meals each day, plus coffee and bread on demand. The children often came upstairs to visit, bringing books, games, and laughter. Much to the delight of all, he introduced them to that great American card game, Slap Jack. Their playtimes taught the children a little English and helped Daniel expand his vocabulary in French.

Daniel was particularly drawn to little Marie. He could not help imagining her to be his own little Maggie. Holding her close, he would close his eyes and picture himself in the cozy apartment above the store on Wabash Street in Topeka, Kansas, USA. Often a tear or two would slide down his cheek as he regretted the time he was losing with his own little girl. "Holy God," he would think, "I pray the suffering and sacrifices of all those wounded and dying in opposition to this evil will not have been in vain."

André, An Elusive Shadow

Andé awakened in a different space: a room with a high window, a decent bed, a clean sink and toilet. He could no longer hear tortured screams. A buxom, white-clad German nurse came twice daily to clean the bullet wound on his shoulder. A white kerchief covered her thick blond hair. Her large hands were surprisingly gentle. She spoke to him softly in accented French. "My name is Hilde Schmidt," she told him. "I will try not to hurt you. The bullet has passed through the muscle, missing the collar bone and just grazing the shoulder blade. The blow to your head has not cracked your skull, but has left a three-corner tear in your scalp and a nasty bruise," she told him as she shaved the area, stitched and cleaned his wounds, and swabbed them with iodine.

Later she brought *müesli*, brown bread, and cheese for breakfast, and bread and a cabbage stew in the evening. She also asked in halting French, "What is your name? Why were you and your friend walking in the forest? Where did you get the guns? Where do you live?"

André would scream at her, "I cannot remember anything! Why do you torment me with these questions?" At other moments, he would be reduced to whimpering sobs, "I remember nothing. I remember nothing."

For weeks, Nurse Schmidt reported daily to Officer Haught. "His confusion is real. He suffers from crushing headaches. I am sure he has a concussion. He cannot tell you anything in his present condition. He is obviously a *Résistant* and deserves death, but torture is a waste of time. Shoot the bastard and be done with him."

"Be patient, my dear Schmidt, and keep up the treatment and food. We will remind him that he is our prisoner periodically; we still have fingernails and toe-nails to pull. He has a mouthful of handsome teeth to drill," Haught responded. "After these reminders, we can charge the generator and light up his testicles. Perhaps that will spark his memory! I believe this young man has information useful to the Reich. I have a feeling he may lead us to our elusive friend, The Shadow."

Weeks passed and André felt his strength returning. Each night he exercised in midnight silence: push-ups from the floor, chin-ups on the windowsill, jogging from wall to wall. He knew the torture sessions would become more and more terrible. One horror story that circulated among the *Résistants* concerned a captured SOE agent whose body was found floating in the Rhône with all the skin stripped off. Soon after, this agent's entire unit was arrested by Haught. None was ever seen again.

When Nurse Schmidt came to his room with stew and iodine one evening, André was, as usual, sitting morosely on the edge of the bed. When she turned to set the food tray on the side table, he stood, grabbed her head from behind, and snapped her neck. The only sound was the crack of vertebrae. He stripped off her uniform, removed his own shabby clothing, and dressed himself in her starched whites. He tied her white kerchief about his head and knotted it under his chin, covering most of his scant beard. Then he pulled on her white stockings and shoes. After shoving her body and his clothes under the bed, he tapped on the door.

The guard posted outside the room during Nurse Schmidt's visits opened the door. André dispatched him with a sharp chop to the neck. He pulled the body into the room, flipped back the blanket and deposited him into the bed. Taking the guard's key ring, André followed the exit signs to the back door of the hotel, found the correct key on the third try, let himself out, and walked calmly down the alley toward the train station. He smiled and thought to himself, "How convenient to have a hotel with a well-marked exit so close to the terminal!" And of course, Aunt Lucile's friendly local *Centre de la Résistance* was only a few short blocks away. He was sure no one would discover his escape until the morning.

Daniel, Return to Action

Before long, Marie began calling Daniel Dada, probably her version of Daniel. No one discouraged her because it seemed so natural. The warrior and the toddler were becoming more attached with each passing day.

The three months of restriction came to an end. Doctor Mason allowed Daniel to begin putting weight on his right leg by walking with a cane. After a couple of weeks he began going up and down the stairs. By Christmas he could walk without a cane with only a slight limp. It was then he told Simone, "I need to find a way to communicate with my headquarters in England. Maybe we can find a way to send a letter, or, if there is a wireless available, I might be able to get a message to my old unit in Lyon. I am well enough now to try getting back by heading for the coast and being picked up by a boat, or finding a guide to take me over the mountains into Switzerland. I would also like to get word to my family that I am okay."

Simone promised she would speak with Madame Lawrence to see if they could design a plan. The two of them decided Daniel should write a letter and send it through the local church to a Calvinist church in Topeka, Kansas.

"Please fetch my boots."

"Of course," Simone replied, and brought the boots from under his bed.

Daniel picked up the left boot, turned it over, and twisted the heel. Five thousand francs hid there, folded tightly in the hollow heel, with another five thousand in the other. "With this," Daniel said, "I believe I can buy my way back to London and leave some to repay Madame Lawrence and help with the Resistance cause here. My job now is to get fit enough to make the trip."

Simone smiled wistfully. "Duty calls. I understand, and our plans just may work. I do know that Marie will miss her Dada. I will draw a sketch of the two of you before you leave."

The following day, Daniel wrote a letter home.

Then he composed a message to SOE Headquarters in London: "*Doodle Dandy. Aching tooth requires extraction. Please advise.*" Now to find a way to send it.

The next morning, Daniel awoke with a start from a vivid dream of parachuting into France, bombing the train north of Lyon, and riding the cabbage delivery truck into the city. He dressed and hurried downstairs. In the kitchen, Simone helped Marie fill her spoon with apricot jam to daub onto a bite of bread, and Madame Lawrence sliced ham for breakfast. "Hold off on the message to HQ. I have a better idea for getting back to my unit," Daniel blurted. "Do you think we could find enough cabbages stored in cellars to make a truck load?"

Simone and Lala gave each other a look and began to laugh. Of course, jolly little Marie chimed in with her musical giggle. "What are you going to do with a truckload of last summer's wilted cabbages?" Simone asked.

"When we first parachuted into France," Daniel answered, "that's how *la Résistance* transported us to Lyon."

"Madame and I have a better idea. Lily and I will go with you by train to Lyon. You will be disguised as our grandfather, Jean DeBauge. We will be taking you to live with your daughter, Lily's aunt, Lucile DeBauge, in Lyon. She leads a cell in *la Résistance* and lives just a short walk from the train station. She has access to a wireless and, hopefully, can connect with your people in Lyon and SOE Headquarters in London. You will wear a bandage around your throat. The story will be that you have terminal throat cancer and you wish to spend your last days with your daughter. You will be mute, and the scar on your throat will be from an attempt to remove your voice box. We must also acquire excellent forgeries of all the cards the Germans now force us to carry. They are obsessed with organization. Every French citizen must carry a work permit, proof of residence, driver's license, food ration card, clothing ration card, census card, birth certificate, and an identification card!"

"This does beat the cabbage plan," Daniel admitted. "But it puts you girls in danger. I already owe you my life. I hate for you to risk yours."

"Nonsense," scoffed Simone. "You are a valuable asset to our cause. We need to get you back in the fight. We will begin practicing your makeup. We will bleach your hair and moustache and dye them gray tomorrow. Louis will help assemble a wardrobe. It is fortunate that you are small and wiry. Clothes that are too large, a slouchy hat, a bent posture, the cane and limp, all will help you look frail and unsteady. No one would ever guess that you are a vigorous young man returning to the business of being a *saboteur.*"

A month passed before all the forged paperwork reached Madame Lawrence's boarding house. On May 21, 1944, Lily, Simone, and Daniel (now Jean DeBauge) boarded the local train for Lyon. They found facing seats in the last car. Lily and Simone sat facing their "grandfather." A Vichy policeman checked their paperwork and tickets. By noon they were in Lyon. The train station there presented quite a contrast from Simone's first arrival in Lyon. SS officers were everywhere, checking everyone. Simone was horrified to recognize the man checking the line they were in as the cruel-eyed monster who snatched Jacques and his mother from the train, Standartenführer Fredrik Haught. She was afraid that changing lines might attract suspicion.

About a dozen people were ahead of them in line giving Simone time to think. She told Daniel and Lily what was happening; then she asked Lily for her lipstick, and applied some to her lips. She donned Lily's beret and pushing her hair under it, subduing the unruly curls. She told her companions, "You two go ahead of me. I will follow as if we are not traveling as a threesome. If I am detained, go on without me. No argument. I have a pill."

When Lily and Daniel reached Officer Haught, he looked at their paperwork and asked, "What is your business in Lyon?"

Lily answered, "*Grand-père* is coming here to stay with his daughter. He is very ill. The doctor says he will not live much longer."

"What is wrong with him?"

"He has cancer of the larynx and he can no longer speak. He can swallow only liquids."

"Take off the bandage. I want to see his throat."

Lily removed the bandage to reveal the scar on Daniel's neck. "This scar is the result of surgery to remove *Grand-père's* voice box. This is why he is mute. The tumor has regrown. He just wants to spend his last days with his only daughter."

"And you are his granddaughter?"

"Yes, his son, my father, was a Vichy policeman. He was shot by *la Résistance* a year ago."

The SS officer returned their papers and waved them on through the gate. Three Lyonnais businessmen were next in line. Haught quickly scanned their papers and dismissed them. Simone was next. She handed over her papers. He looked carefully at the picture on her ID card, then at her. "You have changed since this picture was taken," he observed.

"I would not have thought it possible, but you are uglier and more vicious-looking than ever," Simone thought to herself. "Yes," she admitted. "As you can see, it is over four years old. Our small village does not have an agency to get a new one. I thought I might update it while I am here in Lyon."

"What is your business here?"

"I am an artist. I have been invited to teach a seminar in drawing at the University here. My students are to create German victory posters for buses and public buildings in Paris and Lyon. I will be here for six weeks."

Simone saw not one flicker of recognition. He returned her papers and waved her on through the gate. She was unaware that Officer Haught's gaze followed her as she walked calmly through the gate and down the street and turned left at the corner. "Simone Bouret," he mused to himself. "Why do I recognize this name?" He made a note to himself to do some looking into this young woman's background. He would send someone to the University to check on her story.

Lily and Daniel were waiting at the corner. They walked on at a pace that made allowance for poor old *Grand-père's* infirmity until they reached Aunt Lucile's home. She greeted them warmly and sat them down to a meal of hearty beef stew and crusty bread. They filled her in on Daniel's story.

"Do you have access to a wireless?" Daniel asked.

"Yes," Lucile answered. "But I am far from expert at operating it."

"I can do it. I am clumsy and slow," Daniel admitted, "but I can make myself understood. I need to make contact with my unit here in Lyon or Headquarters in London."

"I will send for a wireless and an operator," she said. "We keep the operators on the move as the Gestapo has locator vans patrolling constantly. We can probably have the unit and an operator here in a day or two. In the meanwhile, I suggest you stay here indoors, keep up the disguise, and be patient. The girls can explain your cover story, in case we have visitors. I think it would be wise for Lily and Simone to wait a few days before they return to Le Chambon. Simone has told me about her experience with Officer Haught on the train from Paris, and *la Résistance* is also aware of his reputation at Hôtel Terminus. To be safe, I plan to arrange new identities for them, complete with disguises, just in case he has any suspicions."

Two days later, just after dark, the wireless operator arrived at Aunt Lucile's back door. Carrying her machine in its suitcase, she gave a coded knock and the appropriate pass phrase to the maid who answered the door. The operator was Alice Upstill. She did not recognize Daniel until he spoke her name and gave her a huge bear hug.

"Bertie and I were sure you were dead. He saw you fall, but by the time he got to the spot where you went down, the Resistance chaps must have already hauled you away. Thank God you are safe."

"Where is Bertie? Is he okay?"

"Well, he's as okay as Bertie will ever be. I've always thought he's a little cracked."

"I can guarantee more than a little. I was standing behind him once when the wind lifted his kilt."

"Oh, I am so glad to see you, gimpy leg and all! You always make me laugh, and you make a fine-looking, dying old man. Now let's get to work on your message to London. The message was short and simple and, of course, in code: "Still doodling. Next?"

Soon a coded message came from HQ that SOE had arranged an extraction for agent Doodle Dandy. Daniel was to make his way overland from Lyon to the coast of Brittany to a cove on a bay called *Beg an Fry*, a secluded inlet, free of shoals with a smooth beach. Here he would rendezvous with a sleek Motor Gun Boat (MGB 664). A sailor from the MGB would row to shore in a camouflaged dinghy, pick up Daniel, and deliver him to the boat, which would make the six-hour trip back to the Devonshire Royal Navy Base at Portsmouth, England. From there, in a matter of hours he would be back in London. Churchill needed him for a top-secret mission vital to victory for the Allies. Unfortunately, the extraction was not as simple as it sounded. First, he had to get to Brittany.

At nearly the same time, SOE Headquarters in London was sending a cryptic telegram to the apartment above the grocery store on Wabash Street in Topeka, Kansas:

```
Mrs. Hagelman, Your husband found
alive by the French Resistance. Stop.
More information when available. Stop.
```

Sharp little Alice came up with a workable plan. Her suggestion was to contact André Jabot. He was an expert in planning guided tours. "If anyone can get you back to England," Alice stated, "it's our friend André."

Alice wired a message to the loft above the restaurant, *Le Lyon*. In code, she told Bertie to get in touch with André Jabot. The next morning, a large nurse in a rumpled uniform appeared at Aunt Lucile's. André smiled through a scruffy beard and announced, "I am famished for one of Lucile's excellent *crêpes*!" Alice gasped when she noticed his missing fingernails. Preparations for the trip to Beg an Fry would take several days.

After *crêpes* and coffee, André explained Alice's plan. "In a recent raid, the Resistance captured a German military motorcycle with side car. The motorcycle will be trucked here to Aunt Lucile's and hidden inside the house. Daniel, you will become a private in the German Army and designated motorcycle driver. I will assume the uniform and arrogant attitude of a German courier carrying classified documents to a command post on the coast of Brittany. We will acquire appropriate German

Army uniforms. Identification papers and orders for our mission must be quickly, but perfectly, forged." Next he responded to their questions about the condition of his hands. His story relating his capture, confinement, and escape was much abridged.

The rendezvous with the motor gun boat was arranged and would include prayers for good weather. To the coast from Lyon, a trip of about 875 kilometers, would take three days. This would allow them time to arrive at the extraction point well ahead of the MGB. The operation would take place after dark. A waning three quarter moon at four in the morning on May 29, 1944, would allow enough light to spot the boat as it approached, and they could signal their exact location with a flashlight. Would there be hitches? Hopefully not. Might they be intercepted? Possibly. Were they up for the challenge? Daniel was, and he reckoned André had never in his life backed down from a challenge.

The trip to the coast proved to be surprisingly smooth. In spite of increasing German checkpoints and security, André's arrogant swagger and perfect German convinced even high-ranking officers. In addition, their paperwork was impeccable and their supposed mission urgent. Also, the rumbling of the powerful BMW motorcycle was, as Daniel put it, "pretty damned intimidating!" They spent two days feeling their way through Brittany, using back roads and avoiding villages as much as possible. Although their journey was far from a pleasure tour, the countryside seduced them into slowing down to view a herd of *pie noir* Brittany cattle grazing in knee-deep grass. At dawn one morning, the sound of shooting startled them from sleep. They quickly took cover behind a rock wall. Across the field before them, a hunter and his quick-working red and white spaniel emerged from a morning mist, obviously supplementing food rations with some small game.

The pair arrived at the secluded cove called *Beg an Fry* and set up camp to wait for the gun boat. After nightfall, every half hour, Daniel flashed an SOS out to sea with his "torch." Between messages, the Atlantic, tamed to a placid lagoon in the quiet inlet, echoed the sparkling stars. Cool breezes carried the scent of pine and salt water, and Daniel mused on the irony of the peace of this place in contrast to the violence looming in his future. He longed for the warmth of home and the loving arms of his family. The first night passed without any contact. As they sat in the dark listening to crickets in the moonlight, André said to his friend, "What can you tell me about Simone Bouret?"

"Well, she is beautiful and intelligent. She appears fragile, but she is not. Her nerve is steady, and her heart is loyal to those who earn her trust. Why do you ask?" Daniel responded with a wry smile that revealed he really did not need to ask.

"I believe I am in love with her," André admitted. "Both of us became entangled in this war before we had any experience with love, but in the few moments we spent together, I have felt a strong attraction. It seems that fate has something important in store for us."

"I am sure Simone will grow to be a powerful woman, sensible and strong," Daniel responded. "I think it would be unfair to put any demands on her now. I urge you not to treat her lightly or to take advantage of her loneliness. She deserves respect and tenderness. Also, you need to ask yourself if this is the sort of woman you want. She will never hesitate to challenge you if she thinks you are wrong. You, my friend, are impulsive by nature and ruthless by training. I encourage you to wait until you have some control over both of these traits before you pursue her."

"Thank you for your advice," André replied. "I will consider your words carefully."

The second night, during André's watch, the third message produced an answer, and within minutes they heard the distant mumble of the MGB's engines. Soon a rubber dinghy slid silently out of the darkness. André flashed the torch again and a British sailor paddled the boat close enough for him and Daniel to catch the line pitched to them and pull the dinghy ashore.

Daniel and André shook hands and embraced. "Goodbye, brother," Daniel told his friend. "God be with you. You have saved my life twice, and I hope you never have to again. Next time I see you, Hitler will be dead, and we will share a bottle of wine in Paris. *L'chaim*, to you my friend." He raised his hand as if toasting.

"*Bonne chance*," André answered. "Bring plenty of dollars. I will also want a fine meal in a very good restaurant. *Au revoir*."

"And how does one go about finding an excellent restaurant in Paris?" asked Daniel.

"*Il suffit de faire un roc*," André answered with a smile.

CHAPTER 7

A Plan for Simone and Lily

"You two must have new identities," Aunt Lucile announced to Simone and Lily the morning after André and Daniel began the journey to the coast. "A professor at the University has contacted us that Gestapo agents have been there checking on Simone's story. They are looking for her. They know she might be traveling back to Le Chambon. I think the safest plan would be for both of you to remain here for a month or so. I know you are anxious to return to the relative safety of the Haute Loire and your lives there. You will miss your friends and loved ones, but for now, you are safer here in Lyon, and you can be useful to *la Résistance* here as well."

"When the time comes to return to Le Chambon, I think we should travel to Le Puy en Velay by rail, then go by auto to Le Chambon," Lily suggested. "Haught will be thinking Simone is headed directly back to Le Chambon. We will give him some time to be distracted by unsuccessful searches."

"When we travel back to Le Chambon, we should be disguised as nuns." Simone suggested. "We could be traveling to the abbey there, saying we have been in Lyon teaching at St. Mary's School and are returning to the abbey in Le Puy."

"That is a perfect story," responded Aunt Lucile. "The habits will cover your hair and part of your faces, particularly If you walk with eyes lowered, and we can add some padding to make you look heavier and a little make-up to age you a bit. We must have your documents prepared immediately and get word to Madame Lawrence and the others to abandon the boarding house and seek refuge in the forest."

"Is it possible to reach André to travel with us? He could dress as a priest," Simone asked.

"No," Aunt Lucile said. "I think he should dress as a nun as well!"

When André returned from Brittany and opened the door to the alley hideaway in Lyon, Alice gave him a smile, a hug, and the news that Lily and Simone needed his help. "You are to accompany the girls to the train station and see that they get safely aboard the train to Le Puy. Aunt Lucile has arranged papers and disguises as nuns for Lily and Simone, and you will become the abbess, seeing your charges off to Le Puy.

"Allo, André ," Bertie waved from the stationary bike battery charger. "Sa gud ta see ya 'andsome face, but ya better get a close shave if ya ere ta pass as a sistar!"

"Perhaps you should go, my friend, since you so enjoy wearing skirts," André quipped.

"Nay," the Scot retorted. "I dunna want ta shave the beard. Ma face tis uglier than ma bum!"

Aunt Lucile decided a week later that enough time had passed to attempt Simone and Lily's return trip to Le Chambon. She sent a courier from her home near the train station across Lyon to Old Town to the hideaway above the restaurant. He carried a package for André; inside was the black habit, and the *accoutrement* of an abbess. Also included in the package was a note from Aunt Lucile:

"André, here are your new clothes, including underwear and a pair of slightly worn black oxford shoes. I suggest you wear it all for a few days before the journey and practice speaking in a soft, feminine voice and walking in the habit. There is a pocket for both hands in the skirt front: an excellent place to carry a knife. A close shave is in order. *Bonne chance!*"

The day of the departure, Aunt Lucile arranged for a member of the Resistance who worked as a cab driver to pick up Mother Superior André and deliver him to her home. There Mother Superior André met with his charges, Sister Simone and Sister Lily. After a light lunch, André and Simone were left alone at the table as Lily and her aunt were organizing the disguises and makeup.

André reached across the small table and took Simone's two hands in his. "I know this declaration of my affection for you is untimely, but this war has a way of robbing us of chances to speak. I find I have thought of our brief moments together in Le Chambon often. I think fate has brought us together and that the future holds more for us. I need to know if you feel this connection, too."

Simone blushed, lowered her eyes, and said, "Yes, I feel drawn to you as well, but there are so many roadblocks ahead. You are an aristocrat, a Christian, and have many family responsibilities. I am a Jew and probably an orphan. Also, our futures are not in our own hands just now. I do have great affection and admiration for you, and I also feel the physical attraction I see in your eyes for me, but I believe we must put our feelings aside until this war is over. Perhaps then we will have time to get to know each other better and to explore our feelings for each other."

André drew her hands to his lips and kissed them softly. "You are right. Your first impulse is always to be prudent and careful. Your cool reserve is one of the things that attracts me. I long to hold you in my arms and explore the feelings I am sure lie beneath." At this moment, they heard Lily and Lucile returning. Simone withdrew her hands and put them in her lap. André stood and welcomed the women back into the dining room. Lily and her aunt exchanged knowing smiles.

Lily and Simone went upstairs to transform themselves into two young nuns. André, with Aunt Lucile's help, became a portly, aging Mother Superior. The trio walked the few blocks to the train terminal. Crowds of people were lining up to buy tickets and lug suitcases to departure platforms. Others were stepping from inbound trains and greeting loved ones awaiting their arrival. Adding to the confusion were queues for required document checks. Plain clothes undercover Gestapo officials and Vichy policemen wandered through the crowds watching, watching. Among them was SS officer Fredrik Haught and two French Nazi *Milice* henchmen.

Mother Superior André, Sister Simone, and Sister Lily bought tickets. They found their railcar by the number on the tickets and lined up to show their tickets and identification papers to the officers at the entrance to the car. Chattering in French to Mother Superior André, fluttering hands, and kissing cheeks, Sisters Simone and Lily safely boarded the train for Le Puy.

Mother Superior André stood on the brick platform beside the tracks and waved to the young nuns in the window above as the train began to chug away from the station. He then turned to begin his return to Aunt Lucile's. Lowering his head and tucking his hands into the front pocket of the habit, he was focusing on the walkway before him when he heard a familiar voice. Just to his left, away from the tracks, an SS officer and two Vichy *Milice* had stopped a young man in work clothes. Perusing the boy's paperwork was Fredrik Haught, André's tormentor from *Hôtel Terminus*. Haught began shouting at the young man that his paperwork was counterfeit. The young man bolted.

"After him," Haught shouted to the *Milice*. The two ran after the young man as ordered, knocking down bystanders and shouting for him to stop. Mother Superior André reached out his left hand and grabbed the collar of Haught's uniform. Pulling him off balance, he put his right hand behind Haught's shoulder, shoving him off the platform and under the wheels of the departing train. The turmoil of the chase and clamor of the moving train drowned out the scream. No one noticed. The boy escaped.

"Officer Haught is not here," said one of the Milice to the other when they returned to the spot after the chase.

"Lucky for us," answered the other. "He does not readily accept excuses for failure. Let's shed these ugly uniforms and go back to Vienne."

Haught's mangled body was not found until the next morning. Mother Superior André would soon lose the habit and become again The Shadow, *L'Ombre*, on his way to Paris to help organize the battle for freedom that was to come.

CHAPTER 8

Advance Mission to Normandy

Within twenty-four hours of the extraction at Brittany, Daniel was in Manchester, England, brushing up on glider piloting and preparing to be a part of a secret assault behind German lines in Normandy in advance of the invasion. Within three weeks, the air assault began. These paratroopers, glider pilots, and infantry braved frightening odds. The first wave of an attack was usually paratroopers, whose duty it was to destroy as many as possible of the enemy's defenses against an air landing. Then came the gliders, with troops to seize strategic points and subdue German strongholds, and finally, more gliders carrying equipment and weapons. Of the entire force of aircraft that took these British units into this pre-Normandy action, only one British tug plane and glider were shot down.

The American glider units were not so lucky. Under German General Erwin Rommel's direction, the fields above the Normandy beaches where the Americans were to land were spiked with Rommel's asparagus, poles planted deep into the ground and laced with cable and mines. In addition, the weather was treacherous. In the best of circumstances, a glider landing was little more than a controlled crash. The nose of the glider was hinged to lift back over the plane so that troops and equipment could exit quickly: convenient, but dangerous for the pilots who sat there at the controls in the front end of this flimsy contraption. They called their aircraft flying coffins. The winged insignia these pilots wore sported a G between the wings. Pilots claimed this "G" stood for GUTS, not glider. Nearly half of the American gliders crashed, killing soldiers and smashing equipment. Still, those who survived the landing and the withering sniper and machinegun fire from the hedgerows managed to engage the Germans and help gain control of bridges and roads key to the success of the planned invasion that would liberate France and the rest of Europe.

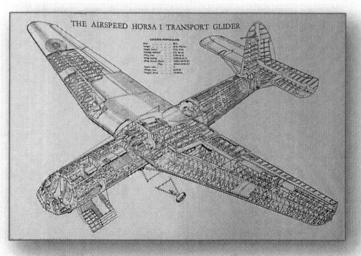

British Horsa Glider poster from Silent Wings Museum, Lubbock, TX.
Photo by Duane Henrikson

CHAPTER 9:
Messages

In Topeka

A uniformed messenger from the telegraph office walked into Hagelman's Grocery at ten o'clock that early-April morning. He asked the attractive woman behind the counter for Mrs. Hagelman. The lady answered, "That would be me," her face draining of color. The young man handed Ida the telegram and waited, hoping for the traditional tip. Her trembling hands tore open the envelope, and her eyes devoured the message. She wilted to the floor, fainting behind the counter.

"Hey, she's passed out!" the telegraph delivery boy shouted. Jacob ran from the meat counter, dropped to his knees, and lifted Ida's head into his lap. Daniel's mother Sarah came from stocking shelves, snatched the telegram from Ida's hand, and scanned it quickly.

"He's alive, Daniel is alive! No other details, but they know he's alive. Jacob, for the love of God, give that boy a tip!"

Two days later, Daniel's letter to Ida from Le Chambon was delivered to the Presbyterian Church down the street. Reverend Hahn brought it directly to Hagelman's.

Daniel and Baby Marie SB

Daniel and Baby Marie

2 March 1944

My Darlings,

With God's help, this letter will reach you. I am alive and well, thanks to the help of the Resistance and my friend André Jabot, a good doctor, and a fine young nurse. I have been in hiding in the South for nearly five months, recuperating from being wounded in a fight with German troops. I have a scar on my neck and a slight limp from a wounded leg, but the entire effect just makes me look even more dashing. My voice is also changed from the wound on my neck—lower, huskier. Think Bela Lugosi without the accent.

Someday when this is over, Ida, we will return to this place. I will introduce you and Maggie to my new friends here, and you will love them just as I do. You will be enchanted by this village and its people. You will walk along the river and drink the wine. Maggie will play with Marie, about her age, whose parents and two brothers were snatched from her by the SS. Maggie and Marie, they could be sisters. In my heart, I think of them as sisters. I am also sending a message to SOE Headquarters in London and trying to make contact by wireless with my unit in Lyon. The plan is to get back to Britain or reunite with my old crew in Lyon. I'm not sure what will happen after that. If they think I will be useful to continue fighting, that is what

I will do. If I do not make it through this next mission, Ida, I have an important mission to ask of you. When this war is at an end, and travel is again safe, please write to the return address on this letter and ask about the safety of Simone Bouret and her daughter Marie. If they are in danger or need help, please do whatever you can to assist them. If they have any desire to come to America, please help them come. I love them both as if they were my own children. Simone has been my nurse and is also an art teacher in the village here. She is the one who drew the sketch I included. It is of me and Marie. Give hugs all 'round from me. There is no way I could love you and miss you more. *L'chaim,* my loves, to life!

Daniel

CHAPTER 10

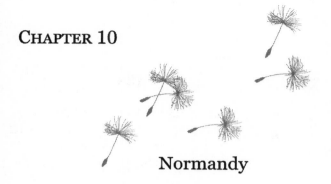

Normandy

As Daniel and his friends prepared for their role in defeating the Germans, another soldier from Kansas, General Dwight D. Eisenhower, and the Allied forces under his command were planning the largest amphibious invasion in the history of warfare. Early on, the Allies chose "Ike" as Supreme Commander of Allied Forces. He did not hesitate to take charge of Operation Overlord, code name for the attack which would take place along the coast of Normandy in early June of 1944. He knew this battle would cost many of his men their lives. He also knew it was the only way to win the war, and that the weight of the resulting loss of life would fall heaviest upon him.

The Germans knew the invasion was coming. Hitler chose his best general, Erwin Rommel, to be in charge of organizing the defense of France's northern coast by building the "Atlantic Wall" which consisted of over 2,000 miles of fortifications: landmines, bunkers, and obstacles in the water and on the beaches. The problem for the Germans, they did not know exactly when or where the attack would come.

The Allies began a massive campaign to confuse Hitler and his generals. The logical place for the invasion was not Normandy, but the narrowest point in the English Channel between Britain and France, Pas-de-Calais. With this in mind, the Allies built a fake army there with plywood planes and tanks and empty tents and put General George Patton in charge of a nonexistent army supposedly in training there. The Germans respected Patton as a military genius and believed that he would be the obvious one to lead the invasion. Even though Patton was, at that time, being disciplined for slapping an enlisted soldier he believed was shirking his duty, Hitler could never conceive that the Americans had actually demoted Patton for such an unimportant incident.

In addition to this subterfuge, misleading wireless and radio transmissions, including, some from Alice Upstill in the hideaway in Lyon, were broadcast hinting that an invasion might come from Norway. André and his *Résistants*, cells of SOE commandos, and shadowy double agents added to the confusion by spreading false information. Even after the Normandy invasion began, Hitler thought it was a diversion and that the real battle would be at Calais, so he refused to bring troops, planes, and tanks from there to defend the beaches at Normandy.

When the invasion began on June 6, 1944, thousands of paratroopers and glider troops were already capturing bridges and roads behind German lines. One of those gliders was piloted by Daniel Hagelman. But Daniel and his crew were not among those fighting for footholds on the ground. His was the one British glider that was shot down.

Daniel, his co-pilot, the pilot and crew of the tug plane, and the fifteen infantrymen in the glider all died in that operation preceding D-Day. They were approaching the drop zone when a German anti-aircraft gun scored a hit on the tug plane. The charge hit the fuel tank and the plane blew apart with such force that the wooden glider towed behind flared like a match. Daniel and the others were incinerated. The ever-present snapshot of Maggie and the lock of her hair in his breast pocket were reduced to ash in an instant.

The invaders from the sea began landing early that morning of June 6, 1944, and by sunset, over 140,000 Allied troops had reached the beaches alive. But the blood of 10,000 more reddened the waters of the English Channel and soaked the sands of the beaches of Normandy; a terrible toll, but half what some generals had predicted. By the end of day five (June 11) 326,547 troops, 54,186 vehicles, and 104,428 tons of supplies were on French soil. By July 4, 1944, one million troops were poised to begin the defeat of Germany. Of course, the next step was to liberate France. Daniel had already given his life to this mission, one among 10,000, but each one of those left behind loved ones: a mother or father, sister or brother, wife or child, who cherished them. Each paid the ultimate price for their loved ones' precious freedom.

A Letter from Topeka

As soon as Ida finished reading the letter from Le Chambon, she sat down and composed an answer on the typewriter in the upstairs office of the grocery store.

Dearest Daniel,

    I must admit, we had almost given you up. When the telegraph boy brought news that you are alive, I fainted! Shock and relief, I guess. We were all in tears and laughing hysterically at the same time. Poor little Maggie could not understand why we were acting so wild. She also did not know whether to laugh or cry. I guess the right response is both! Customers in the store were hooting with us with tears on their cheeks.

    I had no idea Mrs. Hooley could dance. She and the telegraph boy did a jig that rocked the cash register so hard, the drawer popped open. We opened three bottles of wine and passed them around and drained every bottle. People on the street stuck their heads in to see what all the fuss was about and we opened five more bottles. The party spilled outside onto the sidewalk. Officer Ryan began stopping cars to tell drivers the good news. And tonight when the *Topeka Daily Capital* was delivered, the story of your party made the front page along with the news of the D-Day invasion of France.

We are all praying that D-Day will be the beginning of the end of this awful war, and you will soon be in our arms as well as in our hearts. Regardless of the outcome of the invasion to liberate France and defeat Germany, be assured that I will do whatever I can to help Simone and Marie.

Take care, and write again soon.

Much love from home, Ida

Dangerous when Cornered

Adolf Hitler became more and more certain the Allies were planning a large-scale invasion; nonetheless, even after the invasion began, he remained convinced that the battle would be at Calais. He refused to divert his best troops and would not listen to his best generals. He had already lost much of his army, and the confidence of many of his top officers, by wasting time, men, equipment, and money on a winter-long campaign against Russia.

He was also losing what was left of his mind. Hitler removed himself from almost all human contact by hiding away at his mountaintop retreat, The Eagle's Nest, in the Alps of Bavaria, and spent most of his time training his beloved German shepherd dogs and having quiet dinners alone with his mistress, Eva Braun. Not once did he admit to mistakes or take responsibility for the evil of his Final Solution, the attempted extermination of all Europe's Jews.

As the threat of defeat drew nearer, Hitler redoubled his orders to catch and kill Jews. Messages were passed to all the death camps to increase the numbers of prisoners to be gassed, cremated, or shot and buried in mass graves. Jews and *Résistants* in the South of France were no longer in less danger than those in Paris.

Terror in Oradour-sur-Glane

O n June 10, 1944, just four days after the invasion of Normandy began, a company of Gestapo officers, Vichy police, and French Nazi *Milice* paramilitary initiated an operation to destroy a small village, Oradour-sur- Glane, not far from Limoges. The town was rumored to be a haven for the Resistance. Before dawn that morning, the attacking force of about 2,000, surrounded the town and marched inward, squeezing the entire population into the Fair Ground at the center. The invaders took the men from the Fair Ground and herded them into several barns where they were machine-gunned in the legs so they could not run away, doused with gasoline and phosphorus, and set afire.

Women and children had been separated from the

men and herded into the church. Hearing the gunshots, explosions, and screams of the men as they were murdered terrified the women and children, and they began to pray. The troops first attempted to gas them by burning a box of sulfur. When the choking gas failed to kill everyone, the soldiers doused their victims with gasoline and phosphorus, set them afire, and machine-gunned everyone. They then set the church ablaze. The roof collapsed atop charred bodies of mothers holding babies, the town's schoolchildren, and old women clinging to each other. The youngest victim was only a week old.

Less than a handful of over 640 residents escaped. The invaders tried to obliterate evidence of the carnage, but the stench of burned flesh and charred bones was impossible to hide completely. After looting everything they could carry, the invaders set fire to the entire village. All that remained was metal and stone: skeletal baby carriages, burned out cars, charred sewing machines, handleless butchers' knives and carpenters' tools, and crumbling stone walls.

In the end, the invaders found no evidence of hidden Jews or members of *la Résistance*. Two shotguns were discovered: hunting guns, not weapons of war.

Chaos In Le Chambon

The remote village of Le Chambon-sur-Lignon also came into the crosshairs of Gestapo and Vichy police terror. Vichy police raided the local secondary school and arrested eighteen students. A Gestapo officer identified five of the students as Jews and sent them to Auschwitz where they were gassed and cremated. Their teacher, Daniel Trécomé, a cousin of Pastor André Trécomé, one of the leaders of Le Chambon's program to rescue and protect Jews, was also arrested and shot by the Gestapo. Doctor Mason, Le Chambon's physician who had saved Daniel Hagelman, was detained for assisting *le Résistance* and shot on orders of the Gestapo in Lyon. Fortunately, the Gestapo did not arrest his wife Irene, also a trusted member of *la Résistance*, who was in Le Puy visiting her mother.

When Lily and Simone first returned to the boarding house in Le Chambon from the mission to deliver Daniel, they found the house empty. Madame Lawrence and the entire household had fled into the forest. Fortunately, Lily and Simone knew where to find them. They did not stop to ask questions of any of the neighbors or any of their friends at the school. They did stop at the home of Doctor Mason, then headed directly into the woods along a secluded path toward a hut among the densest trees.

A red-eyed Madame Lawrence opened the safe-house door with trembling hands. She tearfully explained to Lily and Simone the details of the awful events that had happened in their absence. "A wireless message from a professor and member of *la Résistance* at the University in Lyon reported that the Gestapo had come to the art department looking for you, Simone, as a suspected member of *la Résistance.* The head of the department tried to cover for you saying that, yes, you had been scheduled to teach some classes in poster art, but you had fallen ill and returned to the countryside. He claimed he did not know what village."

Lily told her, "When we found the boarding house abandoned, our only stop was at the office of Dr. Mason. His trusted wife sent a courier to André Jabot immediately. Knowing the persistence of the German Jew hunters in general, and Haught in particular, we can be thankful we have a safe place to hide."

Here in the forest hideaway, they would wait for André to guide them, or a message from *la Résistance* that it was safe to go home.

PART III

L'Chaim

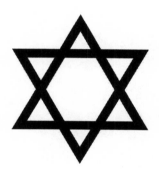

A symbol of Judaism, the Star of David was on the yellow
badges that Jews were forced to wear in the Nazi
occupation of Europe. Today it is commonly looked upon
as a symbol of martyrdom and heroism.

CHAPTER 1

A Message from the Shadow

D elivered by courier to the safe-house in the forest near Le Chambon:

27 August 1944

My Dear Friend,

I am writing to you from Paris. Soon after we arrived here, a message came from the SOE office in London, directly from Général Charles de Gaulle himself, a message that an uprising was in the making, in spite of Allied Commander General Eisenhower's reluctance to back a battle for Paris at this time. In my head, I understood Eisenhower's reluctance to risk men and supplies that could be used to get at Hitler. In my heart, I knew the people of France needed to retake Paris as a matter of national pride and identity. De Gaulle also knew that the citizens of Paris were eager for a fight, and that once the battle began, the Allies must support it. Above all, la Résistance was determined to free Paris immediately. And there was no holding back la Résistance. Once the snake is poised, there is no way to deter the strike!

I and other leaders of the SOE helped organize the battle plan. The gendarmes of Paris were on our side. The battle began with them leading a general strike. The policemen went home, shed their uniforms and returned en masse to the Prefecture on the Îsle de la Cité. Résistance members were dispatched to Notre Dame to raise the Tricolore and ring the bells to announce the battle to all citizens. For days, members of la Résistance had risked their lives pasting fliers to buildings and buses calling the citizens to arms.

Many other fighters from Lyon traveled north to join the battle. In fact, Résistance fighters from all over France hurried to Paris. You should have seen them! They came on tractors, in horse-drawn wagons, on foot pushing old rifles in baby carriages, riding bicycles, even in battered autos rigged to burn wood rather than petrol.

Excitement crackled like electricity. The day we arrived, Alice and Bertie joined a group who spent all night emptying wine bottles and filling them with gasoline, knowing that two or three of those Molotov cocktails would take out a Panzer. (With Bertie in on the project, I'm sure not all the wine went into the gutters.)

In the streets of Paris, citizens, some of them

children, dug cobbles
from the streets,
stacking barricades
against the German
Panzers. I can
imagine it as a
scene from the
Revolution of 1789!
Some cafés and
other street-side

businesses even sold spots for citizens to welcome
the Allies when they entered a free Paris.

The morning of 25 August, Dietrich von Choltitz,
Hitler's military governor, surrendered. Although
ordered by Hitler to wire every bridge and each of
the landmark buildings, even Notre Dame and
the Eiffel Tower, Von Choltitz refused, not wanting
to be judged by history as the man who left Paris
in ruins. The next day, the Allies entered in force,
parading through the city to the cheers of throngs
of citizens. But the victory belonged to us, the
people of France who resisted. Someone snapped
a picture as a British photographer picked up a
child and the crowds cheered. I clipped it from
the newspaper because it reminded me of Marie.
God save the children! Many have died on both
sides in this battle. But Paris is again Paris. For the
first time in four years we sing *La Marseillaise* in the
streets!

I trust this message will reach you soon. Still be vigilant. The war will soon be over, but there is chaos and suffering yet to come. The rule of law must be reestablished. There have been executions without trial of some Frenchmen accused of collaboration with the Nazis, and some women thought to have consorted with the enemy have been accosted and their heads shaved. Again, be vigilant. But I also must tell you that <u>you</u> <u>no</u> <u>longer</u> <u>need</u> to <u>fear</u> Haught. He has relocated to the fires of Hell. I pray that The Shadow has died with Haught. I long to be able to discard this part of myself as I have discarded Haught.

Soon I hope to see my family. To keep them safe, I had to separate from them. Any contact would have put them in great danger. It was important to keep my true identity secret. I have learned from SOE contacts that they are well. As soon as the Germans quartered in the château are gone, I will hurry north to reunite with them. Vivre la France, Vivre la Résistance!

I send my affection with the hope we too will meet again soon,

Fondly, A.

CHAPTER 2

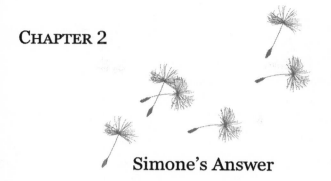

Simone's Answer

Le Lyon Restaurant
in Lyon, France. Tenant, 3ʳᵈ floor

28 September 1944
From Le Chambon-sur-Lignon

My friend,
I pray daily for an early winter. The winters and bad roads of the plateau isolate us, but they have proven to be our friends, also offering protection. The recuperating German soldiers from the hotel are gone. The checkpoints to the north are unmanned. The Vichy police and Milice have left, or melted into the forest and disappeared. I suspect that some are now re-emerging, claiming to be part of la Résistance!
You may have already heard through official channels the sad news that Daniel Hagelman was killed during a glider mission in advance of the invasion at Normandy. His tug plane and the

glider he was piloting were shot down and all aboard both aircraft were killed. I am certain that all who knew him—friends, family, comrades—will mourn his death and remember his bravery. It is hard to imagine that such a kind heart could also be a fierce fighter. I believe the answer lies in his determination to defend those he loved.

Marie and I have returned with Madame Lawrence and the rest of the household to her boarding house above the square. We are again warm and well fed, but the atmosphere in Le Chambon-Sur-Lignon is much changed. The nonviolent influence of Pastor Trécomé has disappeared. Many young men of the village now call themselves Maquisards and strut about in makeshift uniforms carrying assorted weapons, looking for Germans to kill.

Those who have dedicated themselves to saving children remain faithful to their calling, but their work is far from done. A few Jewish parents have come looking for their children, but the younger ones do not recognize their mothers and fathers. Many reunions are far from joyous and prove to be difficult for all concerned. Imagine more tears than smiles, more pain than joy. Tragically, even more children, especially the older ones who remember their families, are now faced with knowing that their mothers and fathers, brothers and sisters will <u>never</u> come.

I am among these. It has been more than a month now since Paris was freed, and I have heard nothing from my parents. I fear the worst. As soon as order returns, I will come to Paris and my former home. If I do not find my parents, I will not reclaim the house. I fear there are many tears to shed. I have contacted my father's banker friend in Switzerland, and he assures me that my funds are safe and available whenever I need them. It appears that I am wealthier than I ever dreamed of being. I have been giving a great deal of thought to the future.

When Lily and I were first traveling from Lyon to Le Chambon, we passed a house on the river in the countryside near Vienne. The house stood above the bank of the Rhône, a grand house with peaked roofs and turrets. I drew a quick sketch of it as we passed. I have thought of it many times since my

La Maison des Revés

first view. I dream of buying this house and starting a school for children victimized by this war. It will be a place filled with books, art, music, learning, and love. Those who have forgotten love will find it in abundance here in this place. I will adopt Marie and we will build a life for ourselves and others in need of healing in our house of dreams, our Maison des Revês.

I have written to Daniel Hagelman's family and invited them to visit when peace returns. I am convinced that we share a connection worthy of nurture. I believe in Daniel's idea that these two girls, his Maggie and my Marie, are daughters of his heart. I will do whatever I can to bring us all together. Ida, Maggie's mother, has written to us asking about our situation and informing us of Daniel's death. I feel I have lost a well-loved older brother. I can envision a time when Ida and Maggie will come. I am sure we will all be instant friends.

When your life allows, come to me. We have much to learn about each other, and how our lives may someday fit together. I am sure that whatever fate has in store for us will be positive. We will always share a history and a friendship. I also pray that your family is well and safe.

> *With love,*
> *no longer Simone Bouret,*
> *but again myself and always*
> *your friend, Rachel Ropfogel*

Epilogue, June 6, 2019

Long after World War II was over, arm-in-arm, tears wetting their cheeks, two dear old friends, close as sisters, stood before a Star of David marking Daniel Hagelman's grave in the vast cemetery above the beaches at Normandy.

"This view always moves me to tears," Maggie Hagelman remarked, taking in the rows and rows of markers stretching to the horizon.

"Yes, no matter how often we visit, the numbers of those who died always overwhelms me," said Marie Ropfogel-Jabot, wiping her eyes.

"And this visit is particularly moving. To think it is seventy-five years today that all of these buried here gave their lives for our freedom," Maggie added.

"Yes," Marie nodded as she whispered, "Rest easy, dear Dada. We know you and the others did not die in vain."

Maggie turned to Marie. "Hitler and his vile plan have scattered our people like so many seeds blown into the wind. A few like Dada lie here. Millions more perished in the ovens of the camps. Some, like us, found fertile soil and survive. My tears are for all who died and all who loved them. My fear is that we still struggle against the evil that caused all this suffering. I pray that fear and hate will never again tear any child anywhere from a parent's arms."

Marie wiped her eyes once more and added, "Sometimes I wonder if any war is ever really over. Again, we see images of children in cages. Again, it becomes a time for tears. All these years later we still work for sanity and peace, and raise our voices against bigotry and injustice. Thank Heaven we can always return to Maman Rachel's *Maison des Revês*, her house of dreams."

"*L'chaim*, my dear sister, *l'chaim*," said Maggie, and she wrapped Marie, also the daughter of her father Daniel's heart, into a tight, warm hug.

And So the Story Ends

In his late thirties, André Jabot, *L'ombre*, hero of *la Résistance* in France during World War II, began to suffer from severe headaches, seizures, and hallucinations. Haunted by shadows in his own soul, André's condition deteriorated until he required hospitalization. He died in 1967 from dementia as a result of brain trauma suffered during the war. He was 44 years old.

After the war, Rachel and André Jabot and daughter Marie lived Rachel's dream in the tall house on the Rhône. Throughout the rest of her life, Rachel continued to use her skills as a teacher of art, dedicating herself to rescuing children, regardless of race or religion. The war took her parents, her childhood, and her husband, but never her generous spirit or capacity for love. As the years passed, she became a fixture in the nearby town of Vienne, taking daily walks, doing her shopping, always tastefully dressed. On July 19, 2019, at age 94, Rachel died peacefully in her home, the school still standing above the mighty Rhône.

Background Material

Daucé, Emmanuel, Frédéric Krivine, Philippe Triboit. With Robin Renucci, Audrey Fleurot, Thierry Godard, Marie Kremer. *A French Village.* Television Series. 2009-2017.

Hébras, Robert. David Denton trans. (2001). *The Tragedy Hour by Hour.* Saintes, France: Le Chemins de la Mémoire.

Kix, Paul. (2017). *The Saboteur.* New York: Harper Perennial.

Moorhead, Caroline. (2014). *Village of Secrets.* New York: Harper Perennial.

Pearson, Judith L. (2005). *The Wolves at the Door.* Gilford, Connecticut: The Lyons Press.

Is Paris Burning? Director René Clément. Paramount Pictures. 26 October 1966. Motion picture.

Conversations with German and French citizens on our trips abroad provided true life accounts of their experiences during WWII. Their reminiscences added a sense of reality to my characters and their experiences. Remembered conversations with my family throughout my childhood led to my desire to write *A Time for Tears.*

My husband Duane and I and our friend Amanda Mendoza and her aunt, Bren Geerinckx-Rice spent two weeks in France in May and early June of 2019, traveling to Lyon, Vienne, Le Chambon-sur-Lignon, Le Puy en Valle, Vichy, and Oradour-sur-Glane gathering information and impressions of places in the story.

The character of André Jabot is loosely based upon the historical Resistance leaders and SOE members, French aristocrat and master spy Robert de La Rochefoucauld and American diplomat-turned-spy Virginia Hall.

The beginning of my story is inspired by a scene in Episode One, Season One, of the French TV series, A French Village.

Permission to use the photo of photographer and child in Andre's letter : This image was created and released by the Imperial War Museum on the IWM Non Commercial License. Photographs taken, or artworks created, by a member of the forces during their active service duties are covered by Crown Copyright provisions. Faithful reproductions may be reused under that license, which is considered expired 50 years after their creation.

Acknowledgments

My friend Marjorie Witt Werly helped tremendously gathering background material. She also shared stories about her father Keith Witt's experiences in WWII as a glider pilot. She has been a staunch cheerleader throughout the long process of creating this story.

Amanda Mendoza, friend and fellow lover of France and veterinarians, helped us plan and execute a road trip through central France, enriching my feeling for village life and giving depth to background and description. She also edited and suggested additional phrases in French to add authenticity to my text.

Thanks to Becca Resner for a helpful early edit.

Special thanks also to my friend Sharon Stephens who read several iterations and provided editing and helpful observations and suggestions. Thanks to my sharp-eyed friends Jean-Ellen Kegler and Marcia Lawrence. Both helped with thorough final editing.

Also thanks to my cadre of buddies who have read excerpts and provided support.

Artist Elizabeth Daniel provided the sensitive and appropriate illustrations for Rachel's diary.

I owe special appreciation to Carmaine Ternes, editor and reviewer, and Tracy Million Simmons of Meadowlark Press, publisher, for their professional services and friendship.

Above all others, I thank my husband Duane Henrikson, retired veterinarian and amazing photographer, for putting up with and fixing my impatience with all things computer. I am grateful for his love and his lovely photographs. He also drove us all over central France, found great Air B&Bs and enjoyed doing it.

Jerilynn Jones Henrikson, 2020

About the Cover

Tracy Million Simmons of Meadowlark Press chose to use my husband Duane Henrikson's photo of the house on the Rhône I had fallen in love with during a trip to France in 2018. In this story my heroine Rachel notices the same house on her journey to Le Chambon. In her mind it becomes a dream sanctuary for life after the war.

A little research to find out more about the house by way of a letter to the village of Sainte Colombe where the house is located gave this answer:

> Hello Madam,
> In 1642, the Order of the Visitation of Holy Mary bought a bowling green and an archery site to build a convent. At their command, in 1700, Mathieu Rozier (architect) built a huge boarding school for young girls of "good families", a cloister with wells, and a chapel, along the path of the Rive-Gier-which became St. Mary's Street. At your disposal for further information.
> Take care of yourself.
> Kindly, Olivier G.
> *(translated from French by Amanda Mendoza)*

What an amazing coincidence that a building I noticed by chance and imagined as a school, was actually built to be a school for girls 320 years ago.

Jerilynn Jones Henrikson, Author

About the Author

J erilynn Jones Henrikson has lived her life loving the rolling Flint Hills of East Central Kansas. The far horizons, changing seasons, and fascinating wildlife of this expanse of prairie have inspired her stories and defined her sensibilities. Most of her writings are designed to appeal to the very young with clever rhymes and engaging situations featuring this place as background. This story is a departure. Listening to her father's experiences and remembering his return from WWII raised questions that, with time, grew into a demanding desire for answers. What was the impact of this War on children her own age who found themselves in the middle of conflict? When she began to feel parallels developing in our current political world echoing the situations that brought about that war 75 years ago in Europe, she felt compelled to write this story. The book, a result of research, memories, and imagination, is designed to inform Young Adult readers of today about this terrible *Time for Tears.*

For Discussion

1. Create another title for this story. Explain your choice.

2. Choose a character and find a quote that helps define that character's personality.

3. Explain the motivation of each: Daniel Hagelman, André Jabot, and Rachel Ropfogel for becoming members of the Resistance. Which of the three do you see as the main character of the story? Explain.

4. If you were to move to France, which location would you pick for your home? Why?

5. Give three examples where the author lightens the mood with humor.

6. You are giving a dinner party with a French theme. What would you serve?

7. Write a poem or draw a sketch inspired by a favorite scene.

8. Think of someone you know who has been affected by living through or serving in war time. How was that person affected by that experience?

9. What parallels do you see between the timeframe of this story and today?

10. Define "theme" as a literary term and write a theme statement for this story.

Read

A Meadowlark Book

Nothing feels better than home

While we at Meadowlark Books love to travel, we also cherish our home time. We are nourished by our open prairies, our enormous skies, community, family, and friends. We are rooted in this land, and that is why Meadowlark Books publishes regional authors.

When you open one of our fiction books, you'll read delicious stories that are set in the Heartland. Settle in with a volume of poetry, and you'll remember just how much you love this place too—the landscape, its skies, the people.

Meadowlark Books publishes memoir, poetry, short stories, and novels. Read stories that began in the Heartland, that were written here. Add to your Meadowlark Book collection today.

Specializing in Books by Authors from the Heartland Since 2014

WWW.MEADOWLARK-BOOKS.COM

Specializing in Books by Authors from the Heartland since 2014

Made in the USA
Columbia, SC
11 October 2020